Uncovering Truths in Notting Hill
ECHOES OF IDENTITY
Revelations Await

Copyright © 2024 Edi Gonzalo

All rights reserved.

ISBN: 9798333713995

© VividArt Studios

We invite you to continue your literary journey by exploring our collection of books. Discover new perspectives, unlock fresh stories, and add more hues to your imagination.

Follow us on
Instagram

◉ *vividart.studios*

This book was created by Edi Gonzalo and released by Vivid Art in collaboration with Amazon

CONTENTS

PROLOGUE 7

CHAPTER 1 11
Introduction & Richard's Life in Bath

CHAPTER 2 20
The Notting Hill House and the Thornton Family

CHAPTER 3 35
Richard's Relocating to London, James hired and family dilemmas

CHAPTER 4 69
Unearthing the Past

CHAPTER 5 86
David is hired & James's and David family dilemmas

CHAPTER 6 111
James's secret affair

CHAPTER 7 163
Final project and house conclusion

ABOUT THE AUTHOR 183

PROLOGUE

❖

In the heart of London, where the city's rhythm reverberates through bustling streets, a tale unfolds against the backdrop of mystery, history, personal discovery, and LGBTQ+ themes.

Echoes of Identity invites you to embark on a captivating journey, delving into a historical house in Notting Hill, a century-old marvel acquired by the Thornton family.

Meet Richard Cutler, a seasoned architect who relocates from the quiet city of Bath to embark on a grand architectural project in the vibrant district of Notting Hill. Joining him are James Turner, a skilled craftsman from Leeds, and David Mitchell, a Londoner from Soho who often finds himself mediating between Richard's grand visions and

James's meticulous nature. Their collaboration on refurbishing a historic house becomes the foundation for an unexpected bond, complicated by their countryside origins and the bustling cityscape of London.

However, Echoes of Identity delves deeper than architectural endeavours, exploring personal landscapes. Amidst ambition and possibility, James reveals a clandestine affair from his teenage years, shaping his identity and intertwining it with the broader narrative.

In the interconnected tapestry of life, Richard's marriage to Sarah represents the beauty of committed love, while James's union with Emily exudes youthful vibrancy. Meanwhile, David, navigating London solo, embodies independence and adventure. Though their paths diverge, each character contributes to the rich fabric of human experience, illustrating different facets of relationships and individual journeys within the bustling cityscape.

The story takes an unexpected turn with the dramatic discovery of human bones hidden within a basement wall, transforming their professional endeavour into a deeply personal quest for truth. The forensic investigation, led by DI Harriet Clarke, reveals a narrative of love, jealousy, and tragedy through Thomas Reed's diary, detailing his tumultuous relationship with Elizabeth Hawkins.

Amidst the chaos, James confides in Richard about the fading intimacy in his marriage, adding a new dimension to their friendship. As Richard, James, and David navigate the restoration, they face increasing danger and unravel the house's dark secrets. Despite mounting risks, their determination to uncover Elizabeth Hawkins' tragic story drives them forward.

At the helm of this architectural endeavour stands the Thornton family, whose legacy and influence shape the landscape of Notting Hill. As Richard, James, and David navigate their personal and professional challenges, they must also contend with the Thornton family's expectations and the secrets within the walls they seek to restore.

Echoes of Identity is a story of hidden truths and confronting ghosts of the past, exploring the balance between preserving history and forging new beginnings, inviting readers to reflect on their own echoes of identity within the grand tapestry of life.

So, take a seat and embark on this fascinating journey with Richard, James, and David. Prepare for an intriguing adventure brimming with mystery, history, personal discovery, LGBTQ+ themes, and plenty of drama. With twists and turns at every corner, this is a story you won't want to miss. Enjoy every moment!

CHAPTER 1

INTRODUCTION & RICHARD'S LIFE IN BATH

❖

In the serene countryside of Bath, Richard Cutler's life unfolds against the backdrop of rolling hills and historical charm. A seasoned architect in his early forties, Richard's portfolio mirrors the timeless beauty of his surroundings. His salt-and-pepper hair, a mix of dark strands and streaks of grey, speaks of wisdom accumulated over the years. Standing tall at 6 feet 2 inches, his commanding presence is accentuated by a sharp jawline and piercing blue eyes.

Richard is well-known professionally in Bath for his meticulous attention to detail and his ability to blend modern design with historical elements. His architectural firm, Cutler & Associates, occupies a quaint office in the heart of Bath. The office itself is a testament to Richard's design philosophy—a harmonious blend of contemporary aesthetics and classical architecture.

Richard's heart is deeply intertwined with his family. His wife, Sarah Cutler, an accomplished lawyer in her late thirties, provides insights into the career opportunities that might arise in the bustling city. Her tailored business attire conceals quiet uncertainties beneath her poised exterior, with shoulder-length chestnut hair framing high cheekbones and a determined expression.

The Cutler family is completed by their two teenagers, Alex and Olivia, both 17 years old. The twins navigate the turbulence of adolescence, adding a layer of complexity to family dynamics. Alex, a budding musician with a rebellious streak, sports a messy hairstyle that mirrors his desire for individuality, he can often be found strumming his guitar. Olivia, an intellectual and contemplative twin, has a more reserved and classic appearance, she spends her afternoons immersed in books.

Their country life is a canvas of shared moments: family dinners in the cosy kitchen, laughter echoing through the halls, and the timeless beauty of the Bath landscape framing their daily existence. The Cutler Residence, a charming blend of history and modernity, is a sanctuary where the echoes of their lives resonate harmoniously.

Richard's routine in Bath reflects a blend of professional dedication and family life. Each morning begins with a quiet moment of reflection, a practice that stems from the family's regular attendance at the local Anglican church. Their faith is a cornerstone of their lives, providing a sense of community and continuity. Richard often finds solace and inspiration during these early moments of the day, which help him navigate the challenges and decisions he faces.

Weekends are a time for family bonding and exploration. The historic city of Bath offers a plethora of activities, from visits to the iconic Roman Baths to leisurely strolls through the Royal

Crescent. Richard and his family enjoy immersing themselves in the rich cultural tapestry of their city. They frequently attend local events and exhibitions, fostering a deep appreciation for the arts and history.

One of the highlights of their weekends is attending Bath Rugby matches. As passionate supporters, the Cutlers don their team's colours and join the throngs of fans at the Recreation Ground. The exhilarating atmosphere of the games, combined with the sense of community, strengthens their family bonds. Cheering for their team, sharing in the victories and losses, becomes a cherished family tradition.

Richard's reputation in Bath is built on a series of successful house projects that showcase his ability to respect historical integrity while integrating modern conveniences. From restoring Georgian townhouses to designing contemporary additions to Victorian homes, his work is celebrated for its elegance and functionality. His projects often become local landmarks, admired for their seamless blend of past and present.

Despite his success, Richard has begun to feel a growing sense of restlessness in Bath. The tranquil countryside, with its rolling hills and historical charm, no longer offers the professional challenges and opportunities that once fuelled his ambition.

As he gazes upon the familiar landscapes that have shaped his career thus far, Richard senses a yearning to expand his architectural horizons beyond the confines of Bath. His creativity, honed through years of designing and restoring homes in this picturesque setting, now whispers of untapped potential awaiting discovery in broader vistas.

Deep within, Richard harbours a profound belief that his talents and vision are destined for more significant projects and recognition. This inner conviction stirs within him, urging him to seek out new landscapes where his architectural prowess can flourish on a grander stage.

Reflecting on where this grander stage might be, Richard finds his thoughts repeatedly drawn to London. The bustling metropolis, with its rich tapestry of history and modernity, represents the epitome of architectural innovation and challenge.

The city's skyline, a blend of historical landmarks and cutting-edge design, offers the perfect canvas for Richard to push the boundaries of his creativity. London, with its vibrant professional community and dynamic projects, seems to be calling out to him, promising a realm where his skills could be tested and his vision realised in ways that Bath could no longer provide.

Richard's heart races with the possibilities that London presents. He imagines himself immersed in projects that demand the utmost of his abilities, collaborating with like-minded professionals, and contributing to the architectural legacy of one of the world's most iconic cities. The prospect of such professional growth excites him, but it also brings a mix of apprehension and determination. He knows that pursuing a career in London will require sacrifices and adjustments, not just for him but for his entire family.

Determined to act on this newfound clarity, Richard begins exploring opportunities in London. He meticulously prepares his portfolio, showcasing the depth and breadth of his work, and begins the process of submitting online applications to architectural firms renowned for their innovative projects. Each application is a step towards a new future, filled with anticipation and hope that London will indeed be the place where his career can reach new heights. The uncertainty of waiting for responses becomes a backdrop for his internal conflict as he weighs the allure of professional growth against the stability of the life they have built in Bath.

As the days pass, Richard finds himself checking his email with increasing frequency, each new message bringing a mix of hope and apprehension. The digital realm of online applications becomes a bridge between his current life and the ambitious future he envisions. Richard's decision to seek out these opportunities marks the beginning of a transformative journey, one that promises to reshape his career and personal life in ways he has yet to fully comprehend.

As Richard pursued a job in London, he navigated the intricacies of online applications, submitting his credentials and aspirations to various architectural firms. The uncertainty of waiting for responses served as a backdrop for his internal conflict, weighing the allure of professional growth against the stability of the life they had built in Bath.

Amidst the virtual sea of applications, one response stood out: an invitation from the Thornton family for an interview. The Thorntons, prominent figures in London's architectural landscape, were embarking on a grand project in Notting Hill. Intrigued by Richard's portfolio and the passion evident in his application, they sought to explore the potential synergy of his skills with their vision.

The invitation arrived on a crisp Monday morning, tucked within a meticulously sealed envelope. The heavy cardstock and elegant script spoke volumes about the importance and formality of the occasion. Richard's heart skipped a beat as he carefully opened it, revealing an invitation to an interview in London the following week.

This unexpected turn of events became a pivotal moment in Richard's dilemma. The prospect of joining the Thornton project and shaping the skyline of London fuelled his passion and ambition. The interview was a professional opportunity and a catalyst for a journey that would intertwine his architectural aspirations with the unfolding chapters of his family's life.

As the story unfolds, Bath's tranquil rhythms give way to the bustling streets of London. Richard's journey captures his architectural endeavours and the intricate dynamics of family, love, and self-discovery against the backdrop of two vastly different landscapes.

CHAPTER 2

THE NOTTING HILL HOUSE AND THE THORNTON FAMILY

❖

The day of the interview arrived swiftly. Richard found himself on an early train to London, leaving behind the tranquil landscapes of Bath. As the countryside blurred into the sprawling urban expanse, a mix of excitement and apprehension settled in his chest.

As the train sped through the changing landscapes, Richard gazed out the window, his mind a whirl of thoughts and emotions. The familiar sights of Bath slowly gave way to the more industrial and densely packed outskirts of London. He couldn't help but reflect on his life back in Bath—the quiet streets, the historic charm, the steady rhythm of his routine. His architectural firm, Cutler & Associates, had achieved considerable success, but the sense of limitation he felt had grown increasingly persistent.

He thought of Sarah and the twins, Alex and Olivia. How would they adapt to this change if he secured the position? The family discussions had been supportive, but Richard knew the reality of relocating would be challenging for everyone. He hoped the allure of London's vibrant culture and opportunities would outweigh the initial discomfort of the transition.

His mind then drifted to the projects he had brought along. Each drawing and photograph in his portfolio represented countless hours of dedication and creativity. Richard took a deep breath, reminding himself that this interview was not just a test of his skills, but also a chance to reaffirm his belief in his own potential. The opportunity to work in London with the prestigious Thornton family could redefine his career, pushing him to new heights.

As the train drew closer to its destination, the nervousness in his chest mingled with a growing sense of determination. This was his chance to break free from the constraints he felt in Bath and to embrace the challenges and rewards that a dynamic city like London could offer. Richard knew that the path ahead was uncertain, but he also knew that without taking this step, he would always wonder what might have been.

When the train finally pulled into the station, Richard gathered his belongings, including his precious portfolio, and stepped onto the platform. The bustling energy of London immediately enveloped him, a stark contrast to the serene quiet of Bath. With a resolute heart and a clear vision, Richard set off towards his interview, ready to embrace whatever the future held.

Richard brought with him a meticulously prepared portfolio, showcasing his drawings and completed projects. These physical representations of his architectural vision and accomplishments symbolised not just his professional journey thus far but also the potential that lay ahead.

Upon arrival, the grandeur of the Thornton residence immediately struck Richard. Nestled in Notting Hill, the house exuded a timeless elegance that mirrored his architectural ethos. Its Victorian façade, adorned with intricate carvings and ivy-clad walls, hinted at the stories and histories it held within.

The house owners in Notting Hill were members of the Thornton family, a well-established and culturally diverse household.

Robert Thornton, a successful entrepreneur, made his fortune through a series of innovative ventures in the tech and real estate sectors. His business acumen was matched only by his passion for preserving historical properties. With a keen interest in architecture and design, Robert envisioned maintaining the house's historical charm while incorporating modern elements to meet the needs of a contemporary lifestyle. His commitment to this vision was evident in every decision made during the refurbishment process.

Eleanor Thornton, his wife, was a well-known philanthropist and an art enthusiast with a penchant for cultural exploration. A curator by profession, she had a deep appreciation for art history and frequently traveled to discover new artists and pieces to add to her collection. Her aesthetic taste was reflected in the curated art pieces and subtle touches of elegance that adorned the interiors. Each room in the house was a testament to her refined eye, with carefully selected artworks and decor elements that harmonised with the house's architectural heritage. For Eleanor, the house was not just a residence but a canvas for her family's shared appreciation of history, art, and life.

The couple had two children, Amelia and Henry, both actively involved in the refurbishment process. Amelia, a university student studying art history, brought a fresh perspective to the project. Her academic background provided valuable insights into the aesthetic aspects of the renovation, and her passion for art history mirrored her mother's.

Amelia was introspective and thoughtful, often seen sketching in her notebook or lost in a book about Renaissance art. She had a keen eye for detail and a deep appreciation for the stories behind each piece of art, which she eagerly shared with her family.

Henry, on the other hand, was a budding architect following in his father's footsteps. His involvement in the technical details of the project was driven by a shared passion for architecture and design. Henry was practical and methodical, with a natural talent for visualising spatial dynamics and structural integrity. He spent hours pouring over blueprints and CAD models, ensuring that every modern addition to the house respected its historical essence.

Henry's analytical mind complemented Amelia's artistic sensibilities, creating a balanced dynamic that enriched the family's approach to the renovation.

Together, the Thornton family's collaborative spirit and diverse talents made the house's refurbishment a deeply personal project. The blend of Robert's entrepreneurial vision, Eleanor's artistic flair, Amelia's historical insights, and Henry's architectural precision resulted in a home that seamlessly integrated the past with the present, embodying the unique essence of the Thornton family.

Eleanor Thornton greeted Richard at the door, radiating warmth and sophistication. Her smile was genuine as she extended her hand. "Mr. Cutler, it's a pleasure to finally meet you in person."

Richard returned her smile. "The pleasure is mine, Mrs. Thornton. This house is truly remarkable."

"Thank you. It's been in our family for generations," she said, leading him inside. "But we believe it's time for a touch of modernity while preserving its historical essence. That's why we were so intrigued by your portfolio."

As they walked through the house, Richard was introduced to Robert Thornton, a man with a commanding presence and an evident passion for architecture. Robert's eyes sparkled with enthusiasm as he discussed his vision for the project.

"We're looking for someone who can blend the old with the new, someone who appreciates the past but isn't afraid to innovate," Robert explained.

"Your work suggests you're the right person for this."

The interview soon moved to the spacious and sunlit dining room, where Richard laid out his plans and ideas. The Thorntons listened intently, asking insightful questions and offering their perspectives. The conversation flowed easily, punctuated by moments of shared excitement about the potential transformations.

As the meeting drew to a close, Robert leaned back in his chair, looking thoughtful. "Richard, we're impressed with your vision and approach. We'd like to move forward with you on this project."

Richard's heart soared. "Thank you, Mr. Thornton. It would be an honour to work on this."

Eleanor smiled. "We also want to extend an offer for you to stay here in the house during the project. It will give you a better sense of its character and history."

After Eleanor's generous offer, she continued with a thoughtful suggestion, "While you settle into the house, Richard, we've decided to stay in a prestigious hotel here in London until the project is complete. It will give you the space and time to work without feeling like we're hovering over your shoulder."

Richard appreciated their consideration. "That sounds like a good arrangement. It will allow me to focus on the project without any distractions."

Robert Thornton nodded in agreement. "Absolutely, Richard. We want you to feel comfortable and have the freedom to execute your vision without any pressure."

With the logistics settled, Richard's excitement for the project grew. The Thornton family's support and trust in his abilities bolstered his confidence, setting a positive tone for the work ahead.

The house, built in 1885, was a timeless masterpiece, blending historical charms with contemporary elegance. Nestled within one of London's most iconic neighbourhoods, it bore the architectural signature of bygone eras while embracing the promise of modernity. Its façade, adorned with classic Victorian features, commanded attention on the street.

A grand entrance with intricately carved wooden details and a stained-glass door hinted at the craftsmanship within. The exterior, draped in ivy and framed by wrought-iron railings, whispered tales of the past, inviting those passing by to step into a world where history and innovation converge.

Inside, the house unfolded into a symphony of spaces seamlessly blending old-world luxury with contemporary design. High ceilings adorned with ornate mouldings, original fireplaces surrounded by marble, and hardwood floors exuded a sense of timeless grandeur. However, these classical elements served as a backdrop for modern accents —sleek fixtures, minimalist furnishings, and large windows—that invited natural light to dance through the rooms.

Living spaces were designed for both intimacy and entertainment. A spacious living room bathed in muted tones offered a serene retreat, while the dining area, with its bespoke chandelier, allowed guests to share in moments of conviviality. The kitchen, a modern marvel, boasted state-of-the-art appliances seamlessly integrated into custom cabinetry.

Ascending the staircase, the upper floors had a collection of bedrooms that echoed the theme of sophistication. High-thread-count linens adorned four-poster beds, and expansive windows framed views of the surrounding neighbourhood. Each room, with its unique character and ambience, spoke of comfort and understated luxury.

The crowning jewel of the house lay in its outdoor spaces, a meticulously landscaped garden that served as an oasis in the heart of Notting Hill. Paved pathways meandered through vibrant blooms, leading to a secluded area where one could escape the urban buzz and find solace.

Returning to Bath that evening, Richard felt a renewed sense of purpose. The following days were a whirlwind of preparation and reflection as he prepared to discuss the opportunity with his family. He knew this decision would impact all of them, and their support was crucial.

Amid the serene countryside, Richard found himself at a crossroads in his career. The prospect of relocating to London and taking on new professional challenges sparked excitement and hesitation. Bath's tranquillity held the comfort of familiarity, but the allure of London's vibrant cityscape became a promising new horizon for his architectural prowess.

Gathering his family around the dinner table, Richard shared the news. "I've been offered the project in London. They want me to stay in the house while I work on it."

The room fell silent as Sarah, Alex, and Olivia absorbed the information. Sarah was the first to speak, her voice steady but thoughtful. "This is a significant opportunity, Richard. We'll need to discuss how this will affect all of us."

Alex's eyes lit up with curiosity. "London? That sounds pretty cool. What do you think, Olivia?"

Olivia, ever the thinker, pondered for a moment. "It's a big change, but it sounds like a once-in-a-lifetime project for Dad."

The family conversation continued late into the night, weighing the pros and cons, and considering the logistics. In the end, their collective excitement for Richard's opportunity and the new experiences it promised won out. They decided to support his move, with plans to visit him regularly.

The following week, Richard returned to London to formally sign the contract with the Thornton family, marking the official commencement of the project. With a start date set just three weeks away, anticipation and preparation filled the air. The detailed discussions during the contract signing reaffirmed their shared vision and commitment to transforming the historic house in Notting Hill.

For Richard, signing the contract symbolised not only a professional milestone but also a personal journey into uncharted territory. As he bid farewell to Bath and fully embraced the opportunities ahead in London, he felt a surge of determination to make this project a testament to his architectural prowess and dedication to preserving historical beauty with modern innovation.

In the weeks leading up to his move to London, Richard focused on organising his architectural projects in Bath, ensuring that everything was in order for his temporary absence. His days were filled with meticulous planning, reviewing drawings, and finalising details with clients and collaborators at Cutler & Associates.

Despite the busy schedule, Richard made a concerted effort to spend quality time with his family. Evenings were dedicated to shared dinners where conversations ranged from practicalities of the move to reminiscences about their life in Bath. He cherished these moments, knowing they would soon be transitioning to a new chapter in London.

On weekends, Richard took his family on outings to their favourite spots in Bath, enjoying the tranquil countryside and historic landmarks they had grown fond of over the years. These outings became opportunities to create lasting memories and strengthen their bond before the impending move.

As departure day drew near, Richard found himself reflecting on the significance of the transition. While excited about the prospects in London, he couldn't help but feel a tinge of nostalgia for the familiarity and peace of Bath. Yet, he was determined to embrace the change and make the most of the professional and personal growth it promised.

The final days in Bath were bittersweet, a blend of anticipation for the new adventure and a heartfelt farewell to a place that had been their cherished home.

CHAPTER 3

RICHARD'S RELOCATING TO LONDON, JAMES HIRED AND FAMILY DILEMMAS

❖

A week later, Richard stood once more before the Thornton residence, this time with a suitcase in hand and a heart full of anticipation. As the door opened, he felt the threshold of his new chapter beckoning. The blending of Bath's serenity and London's vibrant energy seemed to mirror his journey, a delicate balance of past and future, stability and change.

Richard's first impressions of London were a blend of awe and adjustment as he navigated the streets adorned with colourful townhouses, eclectic shops, and the lively buzz of daily life. The city's rich tapestry of culture, architectural marvels, and the palpable energy of urban life left an indelible mark on his senses.

Inside, the house's timeless charm and contemporary potential awaited his touch. The project was not just a professional milestone but a personal transformation. Richard felt ready to infuse the walls of the Thornton residence with his passion and vision, crafting a space where history and innovation danced in harmony.

As he stepped into the house, he knew that this journey in London was more than a career move. It was an evolution of his identity, a new narrative waiting to be written amidst the architectural marvels and bustling streets of Notting Hill.

Notting Hill, with its iconic Portobello Road Market and blend of historic and modern architecture, presented a picturesque backdrop to Richard's professional endeavours. The Thornton family's ambitious project, set against the vibrant canvas of this unique neighbourhood, fuelled his creative spirit and determination to leave an indelible mark on London's skyline.

Richard, with his penchant for precision and an insatiable thirst for creative challenges, saw this as an opportunity to leave an indelible mark on the city he admired.

In the first weeks, Richard focused on assembling his team for the ambitious project. Recognising the importance of having the right people by his side, he hired several key members.

An experienced project manager joined the team, known for her meticulous attention to detail and ability to keep projects on schedule and within budget. Her leadership skills and experience in managing complex refurbishments brought an added layer of confidence to the team.

Richard's solitude was soon joined by the arrival of a skilled craftsman named James Turner. Drawing on the construction project guided by fate, James brought practical expertise that complemented Richard's artistic vision.

Richard Cutler's decision to hire James Turner for the Notting Hill refurbishment stemmed from the recognition of James's exceptional qualifications and extensive experience in building houses in the countryside.

James's reputation preceded him, echoing through architectural circles with commendations for his practical expertise and track record of successful projects.

Having honed his skills in rural construction, James offered a unique perspective on collaboration. His hands-on experience in crafting houses in the countryside promised a blend of traditional craftsmanship and a deep understanding of the nuances associated with rural architecture.

Richard, with his penchant for precision and artistic vision, saw in James not only a skilled craftsman but a valuable collaborator capable of translating his designs into tangible, structurally sound creations.

Richard also sought to build a robust team for the ambitious project, which led to the inclusion of several other key members. He hired an experienced project manager, known for her meticulous attention to detail and ability to keep projects on schedule and within budget. Her leadership skills and experience in managing complex refurbishments brought an added layer of confidence to the team.

For the interior design aspect, Richard brought on board a renowned interior designer with a flair for blending contemporary and classic elements. Her creative vision and understanding of spatial dynamics promised to transform the interior spaces into a harmonious blend of style and functionality.

Additionally, Richard hired a young and innovative structural engineer whose expertise in modern structural techniques and sustainable practices aligned perfectly with the project's vision. His forward-thinking approach ensured that the refurbishment would not only preserve the house's historical integrity but also meet contemporary standards of sustainability and resilience.

James, having recently moved to London for work in the construction industry, became an integral part of the evolving narrative. His arrival, like a missing puzzle piece, filled the empty spaces in the house and sparked an unexpected connection that unfolded in the coming chapters of their lives.

James's qualifications spoke volumes. He is marked by a proven ability to navigate the challenges inherent in building houses within the distinct landscapes of the countryside. His expertise in managing the intricacies of rural construction, from sourcing materials that harmonise with the natural surroundings to implementing sustainable practices, resonated with Richard's vision for Notting Hill refurbishment.

Beyond qualifications and experience, James's passion for his craft and his commitment to excellence resonated with Richard. The decision to bring James on board was not solely practical; it recognised the synergy that could emerge when creative vision met practical proficiency.

James Turner hailed from Leeds, a city in Yorkshire known for its vibrant culture and rich industrial history, a stark contrast to the bustling streets of London where Richard's team predominantly hailed from. Recognising the challenges of commuting and the value of having James's expertise on-site, Richard extended a generous offer: he invited James to stay in one of the spare rooms within the house during the refurbishment in London. This gesture not only facilitated closer collaboration but also bridged the geographical and cultural gaps between them, fostering a deeper sense of camaraderie amidst the diverse team working towards a shared vision in Notting Hill.

As the two embarked on the journey of refurbishing the house in Notting Hill, Richard's decision to hire James unfolded as a strategic choice—one that would not only shape the physical transformation of the house but also lay the foundation for an unexpected connection and collaboration between two individuals with distinct backgrounds and complementary expertise. The fusion of Richard's architectural finesse and James's hands-on rural construction experience became the driving force behind Notting Hill's unfolding narrative.

James Turner is described as having more rugged physicality; standing at six feet, he had a muscular build sculpted by years of hands-on labour in the construction industry. A five o'clock shadow adorned his jaw, adding a touch of casual charm to his appearance. James' warm hazel eyes conveyed a kindness that contrasted with the strength evident in his broad shoulders and strong hands that bore the callouses earned from years of shaping the tangible world.

Amidst the ongoing construction in Notting Hill, the Thornton family paid a visit to Richard and James, their faces beaming with satisfaction at the visible progress of the project.

The grand house, taking shape under their collaborative efforts, received accolades and expressions of delight from the Thorntons. The air was filled with a sense of accomplishment as the family walked through the evolving spaces, envisioning the realisation of their architectural dreams.

As the construction project progressed, the synergy between Richard and James began to shape not only the physical structure of the house but also the emotional landscape within. The story of the two men, each with their aspirations and histories, embarked on a journey where the foundation of friendship laid the groundwork for an unforeseen bond—one that would weave through the fabric of their shared existence, leaving an imprint that even the grandest house could not contain.

In the suburbs they left behind, Richard's wife and James's wife navigated the adjustments brought about by their husbands' relocation to London.

Richard's wife was an accomplished lawyer, her days filled with courtroom battles and legal intricacies. Her long chestnut hair framed a face that radiated both strength and warmth. Her tailored business attire mirrored her poised exterior, concealing the quiet uncertainties that stirred beneath the surface.

James's wife, Emily, was a dedicated teacher in her mid-thirties, known for her strong-willed and determined personality. She approached every challenge with a resolute spirit, whether it was inspiring her students in the classroom or navigating the complexities of family life. Her short, tousled blonde hair and casual yet elegant wardrobe mirrored her dynamic energy. Emily's eyes sparkled with genuine kindness, which endeared her to her colleagues and students alike. However, beneath her warm exterior lay a steadfast resolve that extended beyond her professional life to the heart of her family. In private, Emily's behaviour was marked by sudden shifts in mood and temperament, contrasting sharply with her composed demeanour at school.

Both couples were parents, and their children added a layer of complexity to the evolving narrative. Richard and his wife had two teenagers, twins named Alex and Olivia.

James and his wife, on the other hand, were parents to a young daughter named Lily. Lily's innocent curiosity and boundless energy counterbalanced the challenges faced by her parents. Her presence became a source of joy and, at times, a distraction from uncertainties that loomed in the background. As the story unfolds, the perspectives of Richard's wife, James's wife, and the children move into the narrative, offering glimpses of the intricate tapestry of their lives.

The wives and children, separated by physical distance yet intricately connected, played crucial roles in shaping the trajectory of the unfolding tale. This tale explores not only the bonds between Richard and James but also the intricate family dynamics and the resilience required to navigate the complexities of love and change.

The refurbishment project, guided by Richard Cutler and James Turner, became a collaborative venture that celebrated each family's unique vision while honouring the legacy of those who had come before.

As Richard and James embarked on the refurbishment journey, they aimed not to erase the history embedded in the house's walls but to enhance the narrative.

The house in Notting Hill, a harmonious blend of heritage and contemporary design, stood as a testament to the skilful hands that shaped it and the stories it continued to tell those fortunate enough to call it home.

Collaboration with James Turner, while bringing practical expertise to the project, introduced its challenges and opportunities. The dynamic between the seasoned architect and skilled craftsman added layers of complexity and depth to the unfolding narrative, challenging Richard to embrace collaboration and learn from James's hands-on approach to the construction process.

As Richard faced each challenge head-on, the Notting Hill refurbishment became more than a construction project; it became a test of creativity, adaptability, and the ability to weave a new story while honouring the echoes of the past. The challenges, intricately woven into the fabric of the project, propelled Richard's journey from a seasoned architect to a storyteller, shaping Notting Hill's house into a living testament of innovation and respect for history.

Richard faced a formidable challenge in the Notting Hill refurbishment project, navigating complexities that tested his architectural prowess and resilience. The house, with its historical significance and unique architectural features, presented both an opportunity and a puzzle.

One of the primary challenges was preserving the house's historical integrity while infusing it with modern elements. Richard aimed to create a harmonious blend, ensuring the refurbishment respected the property's heritage while introducing contemporary elements that would enhance its functionality and aesthetic appeal.

Structural issues surfaced during construction, adding another layer of complexity. Richard needed to address these challenges meticulously to ensure the integrity and safety of the house. This demanded a delicate balance between preserving the existing structure and implementing the necessary upgrades to meet modern standards.

Neighbourhood regulations and architectural guidelines in Notting Hill pose additional challenges. Richard navigated through zoning restrictions and community expectations, aiming to create a design that seamlessly integrated with the surrounding environment while pushing the boundaries of architectural innovation.

Amidst these challenges, Richard grappled with the project's emotional and personal dimensions. With its rich history, the house has stories embedded in its walls. Richard had to navigate the delicate task of preserving these narratives while breathing new life into the space.

As James Turner settled into the house in Notting Hill, his skilled craftsmanship became integral to the unfolding narrative. Tasked with contributing to the construction project alongside Richard Cutler, James immersed himself in hands-on labour, bringing his practical expertise to shape the tangible world within the walls of the Thornton family's ambitious endeavour.

His work extended beyond the construction site, as James played a crucial role in the day-to-day activities that brought the house to life. Whether meticulously detailing architectural elements, coordinating with suppliers, or troubleshooting unforeseen challenges, James's commitment to the project reflected his dedication to craftsmanship and the shared vision with Richard.

In the intimate spaces of the house, James's skills resonated as he contributed to the physical structure that mirrored the grandeur of Notting Hill. His work became a testament to the synergy between practical craftsmanship and artistic vision, laying the foundation for the unforeseen bond between James and Richard as they navigated the complexities of their shared existence.

Amid the scaffolding and blueprints of their ambitious project in Notting Hill, Richard found a confidant in James. As the two men shared the intimate spaces of the house, Richard began to unravel the layers of his own life, opening up about the dilemmas that echoed through his family.

In the quiet moments between construction tasks, Richard shared the complexities of family life. He spoke of the challenges with his rebellious son, Alex, who grappled with the upheaval brought about by the move to London. The conflict with Alex became a focal point, a raw expression of the turbulence in their lives as the family adjusted to the unfamiliar rhythms of urban existence.

As the house's structure took shape, Richard delved into the nuances of his relationship with Sarah, his wife. The physical distance and the demands of their respective roles created a void echoing through their family home halls. Richard's honesty with James about the moments of missing his wife and the strains on their relationship added a layer of vulnerability to the bond developing between the two men.

Through these conversations, Richard and James navigated the intricacies of construction and the emotional landscape. Their shared experiences unfolded like blueprints, shaping not only the physical structure of the house but also the foundation of a friendship that would weather the echoes of family dilemmas and personal conflicts. In the quiet corners of Notting Hill, Richard found solace in the unspoken understanding that blossomed between him and James.

The Thornton family's first visit came after the initial stages of the project had already set the course. Their faces beaming with satisfaction at the visible progress of the project. The grand house, taking shape under their collaborative efforts, received accolades and expressions of delight from the Thorntons. The air was filled with a sense of accomplishment as the family walked through the evolving spaces, envisioning the realisation of their architectural dreams.

Their feedback, while largely positive, included requests for changes that had not been anticipated in the original plans. Specifically, they envisioned a larger dining area that would seamlessly integrate with the garden terrace, prompting a reevaluation of spatial dynamics and architectural flow. This unexpected adjustment sparked a ripple effect, stirring underlying tensions between Richard and James regarding the project's direction and the feasibility of accommodating such alterations without compromising their respective visions.

However, as the echoes of admiration lingered, tension simmered beneath the surface. Once the Thornton family left the house, Richard and James found themselves embroiled in a passionate argument about the project and the challenges they faced. The clash of artistic vision and practical execution manifested in a heated exchange of ideas, each defending their perspective fervently.

The once-harmonious collaboration became a battleground of conflicting opinions and methods. Richard, driven by his meticulous architectural ideals, clashed with James, whose pragmatic approach aimed to address practical challenges efficiently. The quiet corners of Notting Hill resonated with the echoes of their disagreements, revealing the complexities inherent in their partnership.

Richard expressed apprehension about compromising the architectural integrity that he had painstakingly designed, fearing that accommodating changes might dilute the project's original vision. On the other hand, James voiced practical concerns about the feasibility of implementing alterations mid-project, emphasising the potential impact on timelines and budget. Despite their differing viewpoints, both recognised the importance of finding a balanced solution that would satisfy the Thornton family's desires without undermining the project's overall coherence.

As they navigated the challenges that arose after the Thornton family's visit, Richard and James found themselves entangled in a battle of visions and a journey of self-discovery. The emotional landscape within the house became a canvas upon which the complexities of their partnership unfolded—a narrative rich with both conflict and growth potential.

In the quiet aftermath of their disagreement, the evolving tale of "Echoes of Identity" delved into the intricacies of collaboration, resilience, and the delicate balance between artistic ambition and practicality. The house, standing as a witness to their shared struggles, awaited the next chapter where resolution or further discord would shape the trajectory of their intertwined professional and personal journey.

To alleviate the tensions from their recent disagreement, Richard and James decided to unwind at a local pub in Notting Hill. The clinking of glasses and the lively atmosphere offered a respite from the weight of their professional challenges.

Richard and James's initial awkwardness melted away as the evening unfolded and drinks flowed. Laughter filled the air as they shared stories, momentarily setting aside the complexities of the construction project. The pub's ambience became a backdrop to the evolving camaraderie between the two men.

Amidst the laughter and camaraderie in the pub, an undercurrent of discomfort seeped into Richard's awareness. James's playful teasing about Richard's looks and the attention he garnered from others left him feeling uneasy, a subtle tension settling beneath the surface. Richard began to wonder if James's comments bordered on sexual harassment, prompting a twinge of concern about his friend's behaviour and motivations.

As the night progressed and the effects of alcohol began to loosen inhibitions, Richard found himself grappling with mixed emotions. He questioned whether James's teasing about his appearance was harmless banter or a subtle form of testing his boundaries, including his sexuality —a thought that unsettled him.

In the haze of the pub's lively ambience, Richard opted to navigate this peculiar moment with a touch of humour, dismissing any deeper contemplation of the implications. The vulnerability that had surfaced momentarily was, for the time being, set aside as the night unfolded in a blur of laughter and shared experiences. The discomfort lingered in the shadows, acknowledged but not dwelled upon, allowing the evolving friendship between Richard and James to weather this unexpected turn in their night out.

The following day, as the remnants of the night at the pub lingered, Richard received a call from his wife, Sarah. Her voice carried a mix of frustration and weariness as she complained about the challenges of living alone and managing the teenagers, especially their rebellious son, Alex.

Sarah conveyed her difficulties in dealing with the intricacies of teenage angst and adjusting to life without Richard's presence. The empty spaces in their family home echoed the strains of solitude, and Sarah sought solace in sharing the burden with Richard over the phone.

The call became a bridge connecting the urban tapestry of Notting Hill to the familiar embrace of their home in Bath. As Richard listened to Sarah's concerns, the complexities of family life resonated, weaving threads of connection and responsibility that stretched across the physical distance between them.

The echoes of family dilemmas reverberated in the aftermath of a night that, while filled with camaraderie, had also left Richard contemplating the intricate balance between professional pursuits and the complexities of domestic life.

Richard planned to visit his family in Bath that weekend. He went to Bath and found solace in the familiar routines of family life. The serene countryside enveloped him in a sense of calm, starkly contrasting London's hustle and bustle. With its welcoming embrace, the family home became a sanctuary where Richard could reconnect with his role as a husband and father.

Richard engaged in heartfelt conversations as he spent time with Sarah, addressing the challenges she faced in his absence. They explored potential solutions and strategies to make the transition easier for everyone, realising that open communication was vital to maintaining a sense of unity.

With the teenagers, Richard navigated the delicate balance between understanding their perspectives and providing guidance. The echoes of the night at the pub lingered in the background, adding an undercurrent of contemplation to the familial interactions. Richard approached the conversations with Alex and Olivia with a blend of empathy and authority, fostering an environment where their concerns could be shared openly.

The weekend became a mosaic of moments—shared meals, walks in the countryside, and laughter echoing through the family home. The nuances of familial connection provided a counterbalance to the complexities of Richard's professional life, offering a respite from the urban tapestry of Notting Hill.

In the intimate spaces of their home, Richard couldn't shake off the echoes of the conflicts that had arisen with James. Seeking a confidant, he decided to share his concerns with Sarah, unburdening himself about the challenges that had surfaced during the construction project. Sarah, the steadfast pillar of support, listened attentively, offering her insights and perspectives on the intricate dynamics at play.

As Richard delved into the complexities of his evolving friendship with James, he found comfort in his wife's understanding gaze. The evolving narrative intertwined professional challenges with the nuances of personal connection, highlighting the delicate balance between collaboration and conflicting visions.

In return, Richard shared with Sarah the project progress, the milestones achieved, and the ambitious vision they aimed to realise in the grand house in Notting Hill. The synergy between architectural creativity and practical craftsmanship unfolded in the retelling, as Richard sought to convey the evolution of the project beyond the conflicts that had temporarily cast shadows on their collaboration.

The conversation with Sarah became a therapeutic exploration, a shared journey into the intricacies of professional and personal life. As Richard navigated the complexities of both realms, the echoes of their discussions resonated within the walls of their home, setting the stage for the next chapter in the unfolding tale of "Echoes of Identity."

As the weekend drew to a close, Richard returned to London with a renewed sense of purpose. The familial bonds strengthened during his time in Bath served as a foundation for navigating the intricate dynamics that awaited him, both in the construction project and the evolving friendship with James.

When Richard returned to the construction site, he found an unexpected scene. Empty bottles of alcohol scattered around hinted at a night of indulgence, and he soon discovered that James was nursing a hangover. The air in the house carried the remnants of a night that unfolded in a haze of camaraderie and excess.

Despite the visible aftermath, Richard chose not to confront James directly. An unspoken understanding lingered in the air, a tacit acknowledgment of the shared experiences of the previous night.

The complexities of their evolving friendship, punctuated by moments of camaraderie and discomfort, were veiled by the silence that permeated the empty spaces within the construction project.

As Richard resumed his focus on the ongoing construction, a subtle tension hummed beneath the surface. The unspoken echoes lingered in the air, leaving a sense of uncertainty about the impact of the night's revelry on their professional collaboration. The evolving narrative took an intriguing turn as the interplay between personal connections and professional dynamics continued to shape Richard's journey within the grand house in Notting Hill.

The next day, with the construction project in progress, James approached Richard, a heaviness in his demeanour. In a rare moment of vulnerability, he confided in Richard about the struggles he faced in his personal life. James expressed discontent with his marriage, detailing dissatisfaction, boredom, and a perceived lack of understanding from his wife.

Voicing his frustrations, James shared his perception that his wife often placed blame on him, creating an atmosphere of manipulation and jealousy. The complexities of his marital struggles split into their conversation, revealing a side of James that Richard hadn't seen before. In the raw honesty of their exchange, Richard glimpsed the layers of complexity that shaped James's life outside the construction site.

James confident to Richard that Emily's mood began to shift unpredictably, and her seemingly steadfast resolve turned into an unsettling intensity. In the past years he noticed she became increasingly manipulative, using her charm to control those around her. Her kindness became a facade, masking a deeper, more sinister nature.

Her interactions with family and colleagues grew erratic, and she displayed a chilling lack of empathy, often deriving satisfaction from the discomfort of others.

In terms of family, Emily still showed moments of genuine care and affection, particularly towards their daughter. She would often engage in activities with her, creating an image of a loving and involved mother. However, these moments were interspersed with sudden and explosive outbursts, particularly directed at James. Her temper would flare unexpectedly, turning minor disagreements into intense confrontations. These explosions left James walking on eggshells, uncertain when the next outburst would occur.

He describes that Emily's psychopathic tendencies become more pronounced. Her once balanced life becomes a web of deceit and manipulation, where her true nature is revealed. She is no longer the pillar of strength but a calculated and dangerous force, balancing the demands of her career and family life with a twisted sense of satisfaction. Her behaviour oscillates between superficial charm, genuine moments of family care, and cold-hearted cruelty, making her a complex and menacing character throughout the book.

As James bared his soul, Richard listened with empathy, offering a supportive presence amidst the tumult of James's emotions. The echoes of their shared experiences, both personal and professional, resonated in the quiet corners of the construction project, binding them together in a shared journey of discovery.

In that moment of vulnerability, the walls of professionalism that had defined their relationship began to crumble, giving way to a deeper connection forged through shared struggles and mutual understanding.

Richard's perception of James shifted, seeing beyond the skilled craftsman to the complex individual grappling with his own demons.

James opened up to Richard about the profound impact Emily's behaviour had on his sense of self-worth and stability. He recounted how her unpredictable mood swings and manipulative tactics had triggered deep-seated insecurities that dated back to his formative years. Growing up in a demanding household where achievement was paramount, James had often felt inadequate despite his successes. Emily's alternating displays of affection and aggression echoed dynamics from his past, intensifying his need for validation and acceptance.

In moments of vulnerability, James admitted that these insecurities had led him down destructive paths in his youth. He confided in Richard about his struggles with substance abuse, recounting how he had turned to drugs and alcohol as coping mechanisms to numb the pain of feeling inadequate.

Moreover, James revealed that he had engaged in both heterosexual and homosexual affairs, seeking validation and intimacy wherever he could find it. These experiences, though in the past, still left him with emotional scars and a lingering sense of shame.

As James shared these deeply personal histories with Richard, he expressed a mixture of regret and relief at confronting his past demons.

Richard, in turn, offered a compassionate ear and understanding presence, acknowledging the courage it took for James to confront these truths.

Their conversation deepened their friendship, as Richard saw beyond James's professional facade to the complex individual struggling with his inner demons.

Their bond strengthened through shared vulnerability and mutual support, as they navigated the complexities of both their professional collaboration and personal lives.

Richard's empathy and encouragement became pillars of strength for James, reinforcing their partnership with a foundation of trust and understanding.

Their conversation marked a turning point in their evolving friendship, transcending the confines of their professional collaboration to encompass the intricacies of their personal lives.

As Richard offered words of encouragement and solidarity, a newfound sense of camaraderie blossomed between them, rooted in empathy and shared experiences.

Richard was taken aback by James's candid revelations, stunned by the depth of turmoil his friend had endured silently. He had never imagined that behind James's confident exterior lay such profound struggles with self-worth and past mistakes. As James spoke, Richard felt a mixture of disbelief and empathy, realising how deeply these issues had affected his friend's life and choices.

Despite his initial shock, Richard remained composed and attentive, a testament to his respect for James and their evolving friendship. He listened intently, offering a supportive presence that encouraged James to continue sharing his vulnerabilities. Richard's own upbringing, grounded in strong family values, had instilled in him a sense of compassion and understanding, qualities that now guided him as he processed James's revelations.

Their conversation unfolded with a poignant honesty that strengthened their bond. Richard's ability to set aside judgment and listen openly reflected his commitment to their friendship and their shared project. As they navigated through James's personal journey, Richard's unwavering support became a cornerstone of their collaboration, transcending professional boundaries to encompass the complexities of their lives.

In Notting Hill's grand house, where echoes of identity resonated with each architectural detail, Richard and James forged a deeper connection. Theirs became a partnership enriched by mutual respect and empathy, where moments of vulnerability were met with solidarity and understanding. Together, they confronted not only the challenges of their ambitious project but also the deeper complexities of human experience, weaving their individual stories into a tapestry of shared growth and redemption.

Despite the occasional disagreements and challenges they encountered, Richard and James stood united, their friendship strengthened by adversity and their shared commitment to their craft. As they continued to work together on the refurbishment project, their bond deepened, evolving into a partnership built on trust, respect, and mutual admiration.

Their journey through the Notting Hill house became a metaphor for their own personal growth and transformation. As they worked tirelessly to breathe new life into the old structure, they also found themselves undergoing a process of renewal and self-discovery.

In the end, the grand house in Notting Hill stood not only as a testament to their skill and dedication but also as a symbol of the enduring bond between two men who, despite their differences, found common ground in their shared passion for their work and their unwavering friendship.

CHAPTER 4

UNEARTHING THE PAST

❖

The history of the Notting Hill House reveals a fascinating lineage of owners and designers, each adding their own chapter to its story. Before the Thornton family, Charles and Evelyn Barclay were the custodians of this storied residence, living there from 1975 to 2005. Their thirty-year tenure brought the property a distinct blend of financial acumen and artistic sensibility.

Charles Barclay, with his background in finance, saw the house as a dual opportunity: a valuable investment and a historical gem. His approach to refurbishing the property focused on preserving its authentic Victorian features while subtly modernising elements to enhance its market value.

Evelyn Barclay brought a different perspective. An avid art collector, she envisioned the house as a living gallery. Her refined taste influenced the selection of decor, transforming each room into a curated space that showcased her extensive art collection. This fusion of finance and art made the Barclays' refurbishment a unique blend of strategic enhancement and cultural enrichment.

Their approach to the design maintained a delicate balance between old and new. Classic furnishings coexisted with contemporary art pieces, creating an atmosphere of timeless elegance. The garden, another highlight, was meticulously landscaped to complement the house's historic charm while providing a tranquil retreat.

When the Thornton family took over in 2006, they continued this tradition of blending the past with the present. Dr. Robert Thornton, a successful entrepreneur with a passion for preserving historical properties, and his wife, Eleanor Thornton, a well-known philanthropist, had envisioned the house as a symbol of their commitment to preserving London's heritage. Along with their children Amelia, a university student studying art history, and Henry, a budding architect, they worked closely with Richard Cutler and James Turner. Their project was more than a simple refurbishment; it was a collaborative effort to honor the house's heritage while making it a comfortable home for a modern family.

Richard and James faced the challenge of integrating contemporary amenities without overshadowing the house's historical essence. Their vision was to create a space where history and modernity coexist harmoniously, ensuring the house remains a testament to its rich past while embracing the present.
The Thornton family, however, was largely unaware of the full extent of the house's history. Despite its outward Victorian charm, the property held secrets that even the Barclays had not uncovered. Built in 1885, the house, a century-old marvel, had witnessed numerous stories and mysteries over its long existence. This enigmatic

past began to surface during the restoration, hinting at deeper, hidden narratives waiting to be unveiled.

The transition from the Barclays to the Thorntons was marked by a shared respect for the house's history and a commitment to its future. Yet, as the restoration progressed, unexpected discoveries added intrigue to their endeavour. Through their unique contributions, each family has woven their own stories into the fabric of the Notting Hill house, making it a living legacy of evolving narratives and timeless beauty.

As the project neared completion, a startling discovery during the demolition of a wall added a new layer of complexity and drama to Richard and James's journey.

It was a chilly, overcast morning when the crew began demolishing an old partition wall in the basement. James, supervising the work, noticed something unusual in the debris—a glint of white amidst the dust and rubble. As the workers cleared the area, it became clear that they had uncovered a set of human bones. The room fell silent, the air thick with shock and unease.

Richard was immediately called to the site. Upon seeing the skeletal remains, his face paled. The project, already fraught with challenges, had now taken a grim turn. They quickly contacted the authorities, who arrived within the hour, cordoning off the area and halting all work.

The police, led by Detective Inspector Harriet Clarke, took charge of the scene. Forensic experts began their examination, estimating the bones to be over a century old. DI Clarke, a seasoned investigator with a keen interest in historical cases, found herself intrigued by the mystery.

As the team meticulously documented the scene, DI Clarke pulled Richard and James aside, explaining the next steps. The house was now a crime scene, and construction would be suspended pending the outcome of the investigation. The news hit them hard; the project's future was now uncertain.

With work halted, Richard and James delved into the house's history, hoping to uncover clues about the remains. They discovered that the house had changed hands several times since its construction in the mid-19th century. It was a private residence, boarding house, and makeshift hospital during World War II.

Local historian Margaret Bennett was brought in to assist. She revealed that during its time as a boarding house in the late 1800s, the property had a reputation for being a haven for London's bohemian artists and writers, but it was also rumoured to have been a place of illicit activities.

As the forensic analysis progressed, several theories about the bones' origins emerged:

1. Accidental Death:
One theory suggested that the bones could belong to a worker or resident who had died accidentally. The 19th century was a time of rapid construction and expansion in London, often with little regard for safety. Workers frequently faced dangerous conditions, and accidents were not uncommon. In a bid to avoid scandal or halt progress, it was possible that a fatal accident was hushed up. Given the era's poor record-keeping and less stringent construction practices, an accidental death could have been hastily covered up. This theory posited that the unfortunate individual might have fallen or been struck by falling debris

during the house's original construction or a later renovation, and their body was hidden within the wall to avoid delay or legal repercussions.

2. Foul Play:

Another, darker theory proposed that the individual was a victim of murder. The boarding house's reputation for bohemian excesses hinted at possible foul play. The late 1800s were a time of social upheaval, and the house, with its artistic residents, might have been a backdrop for intense personal dramas. Perhaps a lover's quarrel escalated to violence, or a dispute among the residents turned deadly. Diaries, letters, and newspaper articles from the period were scoured for hints of scandal or unexplained disappearances. This theory was supported by the discovery of personal items, like the rusted locket, which suggested the bones belonged to someone known to the household, someone whose sudden disappearance might have raised questions at the time.

3. Epidemic Victim:

Another speculation was that the bones might belong to someone who had died during one of the frequent epidemics that swept through

London in the 19th century, such as cholera or tuberculosis. These diseases often caused widespread panic, and bodies were sometimes buried hastily to prevent the spread of infection. Concealing a body within a wall might have been a desperate measure to avoid quarantine or panic, especially if the death occurred in a crowded boarding house where an outbreak could quickly spread. Historical records showed that Notting Hill, like many areas of London, was not immune to these health crises. This theory suggested a quieter tragedy, where fear of disease prompted extreme actions.

4. Wartime Secrets:
Given the house's use during World War II, another theory was that the remains could be linked to the war, possibly an unidentified casualty or someone who had died during the bombings. London during the Blitz was chaotic, and many buildings were repurposed for various war efforts, from makeshift hospitals to command centres. It was conceivable that in the chaos, someone might have died—perhaps an air raid casualty or a wartime secret that had to be buried quickly. The period's records were less complete, and wartime censorship might have prevented

the true story from ever coming to light. This theory added a layer of historical intrigue, suggesting that the house's walls might hold secrets from one of the most tumultuous times in London's history.

With the investigation now squarely in the authorities' hands, Richard and James decided it was best to step away from the site temporarily. The weight of the discovery and the constant media presence took a toll on both men. They agreed it would be beneficial to return to their families until the investigation concluded and they could resume work.

Richard returned home, greeted by his wife and children, who provided a much-needed sense of normalcy and support. James, too, found solace in the embrace of his family, where he could momentarily distance himself from the grim realities of the project. Both men kept close contact with DI Clarke and the Thornton family, ensuring they were updated on any developments.

The Thornton family, who had purchased the house intending to restore it to its former glory, found themselves at the heart of the controversy. Dr. Robert Thornton, a successful entrepreneur with a passion for preserving historical properties, and his wife, Eleanor Thornton, a well-known philanthropist, had envisioned the house as a symbol of their commitment to preserving London's heritage. Their two children, Amelia, a university student studying art history, and Henry, a budding architect, had even started referring to the house as their future home.

When the discovery news broke, the Thorntons were shocked and deeply concerned. Robert Thornton, pragmatic and methodical by nature, was worried about the legal implications and the project's timeline. He had invested not only a significant amount of money but also his reputation into this restoration. Eleanor Thornton, with her keen sense of social responsibility, was more troubled by the human aspect of the find. She felt a moral obligation to ensure the remains were treated with dignity and respect.

The discovery also affected Amelia and Henry. Amelia, a history enthusiast, was fascinated and horrified in equal measure. She spent hours researching the house's past, trying to piece together the life of the person whose bones had been found. Henry, younger and more sensitive, was disturbed by the idea of living in a house with such a macabre history. He had nightmares about the bones and found it difficult to even visit the site.

As the forensic team continued their work, they uncovered more clues that deepened the mystery. A small, rusted locket found near the bones contained a faded photograph of a young woman. This discovery fuelled speculation and media interest, turning the construction site into a media circus. Reporters camped outside, eager for any updates, while conspiracy theories proliferated online.

The community's reaction was mixed. Some neighbours were fascinated, viewing the house as a piece of living history. Others feared the negative attention and potential drop in property values. Richard and James found themselves in the middle of a storm of public interest and speculation, with every step of the investigation scrutinised.

As weeks turned into months, DI Clarke and her team pieced together a narrative. Forensic analysis indicated the bones belonged to a young woman, likely in her early thirties, who had died from blunt force trauma to the head. The locket's photograph was matched to archival records, revealing her identity: Elizabeth Hawkins, a painter known for her association with the boarding house.

Further research uncovered that Elizabeth had disappeared under mysterious circumstances in 1893. She was last seen arguing with another resident, a fellow artist named Thomas Reed, who was suspected but never charged due to a lack of evidence. Elizabeth's disappearance had remained a cold case until now.

A breakthrough came when DI Clarke discovered Reed's diary in the local archives. In it, Reed details his tumultuous relationship with Elizabeth, which is filled with passion and jealousy. The diary ended abruptly with a confession-like entry, hinting at a tragic accident. Reed wrote of a heated argument that turned violent, resulting in Elizabeth's accidental death.

Panicked, he had hidden her body in the wall, hoping it would never be found.

The discovery of the diary was like opening a time capsule, providing a raw and intimate glimpse into the lives of Elizabeth Hawkins and Thomas Reed. The diary entries revealed the intensity of their relationship, a blend of creative synergy and destructive passion. Reed wrote about their late-night painting sessions, their philosophical debates, and their public displays of affection that often turned into public arguments.

One entry stood out: June 15, 1893: Elizabeth and I fought again. Her temper is as fiery as her hair, and my jealousy knows no bounds. She accused me of stifling her creativity and being jealous of her talent. I lashed out, words turning to shouts, shouts to a push. She fell, hitting her head on the corner of the hearth. The sound, the silence that followed—it haunts me. I didn't mean to...

Reed's writing conveyed a profound sense of guilt and panic. He described how he carried her lifeless body down to the basement in the dead of night, dismantled a section of the wall, and concealed her within, sealing the bricks back up, hoping her presence would be forever hidden. His last entries were filled with remorse and a deepening descent into madness, driven by his actions and the secrets he harboured.

The discovery of Elizabeth Hawkins' remains and Reed's diary had far-reaching implications, both legally and ethically. The forensic team, now armed with Reed's confession, could finally close the century-old case. However, the decision to prosecute a dead man posed apparent challenges. Instead, the focus shifted to historical justice—recognising Elizabeth's tragic fate and giving her the dignity she was denied in life.

The Thornton family, meanwhile, faced a moral quandary. The house they intended to restore and live in was now a documented crime scene with a dark past. Dr. Robert Thornton struggled with the idea of moving his family into a place with such a gruesome history. Eleanor Thornton, driven by her philanthropic values, saw an opportunity to turn this tragedy into something positive. She proposed creating a small memorial within the house to honour Elizabeth Hawkins and educate visitors about her life and the era she lived in.

News of the diary and the identification of Elizabeth Hawkins spread quickly, reigniting media interest. Reporters swarmed the house, and the story dominated local headlines. The community's reactions were mixed. Some residents were fascinated, seeing the house as a historical landmark with a compelling story. Others were uneasy, fearing the negative attention and potential impact on property values.

Richard and James had to navigate these turbulent waters carefully. They held a press conference with DI Clarke, where they shared the findings and outlined their plans to honour Elizabeth's memory. Richard, with his characteristic eloquence, spoke about the importance of acknowledging the past, no matter how dark, to understand and appreciate the present fully.

In collaboration with local historians and the community, the Thornton family decided to create a memorial space in the house dedicated to Elizabeth Hawkins. A small room on the ground floor was transformed into a mini-museum, featuring her restored paintings, copies of Reed's diary entries, and historical artefacts from the period. The room also included a plaque that told Elizabeth's story and the circumstances of her untimely death.

The grand opening of the memorial was a solemn but hopeful event. The Thornton family, Richard, James, DI Clarke, and many members of the community gathered to honour Elizabeth. Inspired by Elizabeth's work and life, a local artist created a new piece that was unveiled at the ceremony—a poignant tribute to the woman whose talent and life had been cut short.

As the project resumed and eventually completed, the house stood as a testament to resilience and the importance of confronting history. The memorial became a point of reflection for visitors, a reminder of the layers of life and stories embedded within old buildings.

Richard and James emerged from the experience with a renewed sense of purpose and a strengthened partnership. They had not only restored a house but also brought a hidden story to light, ensuring that Elizabeth Hawkins' legacy would live on. The Thornton family, despite initial reservations, embraced their home's history, turning it into a place of remembrance and learning.

The house, now a blend of modern design and historical homage, attracted significant attention, becoming a symbol of how the past and present could coexist and enrich one another. The experience left a lasting impact on everyone involved, shaping their perspectives on history, memory, and the passage of time.

Richard and James emerged from the experience with a deeper bond and a shared sense of accomplishment. They were ready to face future challenges with the knowledge that they could overcome anything together.

CHAPTER 5

DAVID IS HIRED & JAMES'S AND DAVID FAMILY DILEMMAS

❖

After spending several weeks with their families, Richard and James returned to the house, ready to resume their work. The investigation had concluded, and the site was cleared for construction. The pause had given them both time to reflect on the events and the weight of the history they had uncovered. They were determined to honour Elizabeth Hawkins' memory while completing the restoration.

The bond between the two men grew stronger, forged by the trials they had endured and the honesty they had shared. As they worked side by side, they knew that whatever the future held, they could face it together. The house, with its layers of history and stories, stood as a testament to resilience and the enduring human spirit. Within its walls, Richard and James found a project and a reflection of their own lives—complex, challenging, and ultimately hopeful.

In a moment of raw honesty, James confided in Richard about his struggles in his intimate relationship with his wife. With a heavy heart and a sense of vulnerability, he shared that the spark had faded, leaving behind a void of passion and fulfilment.

James's words were tinged with a mixture of frustration and resignation as he revealed that he no longer found joy or satisfaction in their physical intimacy. The once-fulfilling connection had become a source of discomfort and disillusionment, leaving him grappling with feelings of inadequacy and yearning for something more.

As he bared his soul to Richard, the weight of unspoken truths hung heavy in the air, underscoring the complexities of marital relationships and the toll that unfulfilled desires can take on the human spirit. In this moment of shared vulnerability, Richard listened with empathy, offering a silent anchor of support amidst the turbulent waters of James's inner turmoil.

Richard listened intently as James poured out his heart, his words laden with a mixture of anguish and resignation. The admission that the intimacy in his marriage had lost its allure weighed heavily on both of them, casting a shadow over their conversation.

In the quiet of the construction site, amidst the echo of hammers and the rustle of blueprints, Richard offered James a supportive presence, a silent witness to his friend's inner turmoil. The unspoken understanding between them deepened, transcending the boundaries of mere camaraderie to encompass a shared journey of personal exploration and emotional growth.

In a moment of raw honesty, James confessed to Richard that he no longer experienced pleasure or fulfilment in his physical relationship with his wife. The intimacy that once brought them together had faded, leaving behind a void of passion and connection that weighed heavily on his heart.

Richard's response was one of genuine empathy and understanding. He expressed his sorrow for James's struggles, acknowledging the pain and frustration that his friend was experiencing. With heartfelt sincerity, Richard shared that he had been fortunate in his marriage, finding happiness and fulfilment in his relationship with his wife. He admitted that he had never faced a similar challenge in his intimate connection with her.

This moment of vulnerability and mutual respect they deepened the bond between Richard and James. Despite their differing experiences, they found common ground in their shared humanity and the complexities of love and relationships. Richard's words of compassion served as a reminder of the strength of their friendship and the support they offered each other in times of need.

As Richard and James were engrossed in their heartfelt conversation, their reflections on love and relationships were abruptly interrupted by the arrival of the house owners. The Thornton family's presence shattered the moment of intimacy, pulling them back into the realm of professional obligations and responsibilities.

With a swift transition, Richard and James shifted their focus to greet the Thornton family, their professional demeanour masking the weight of their conversations. The echoes of their shared vulnerabilities lingered beneath the surface, hidden from view as they focused on the matters at hand.

The Thornton family's visit brought a renewed sense of purpose to the construction site; their enthusiasm and support injected new energy into the project. Richard and James exchanged knowing glances, silently acknowledging the complexities of their inner worlds as they resumed their roles as architects and craftsmen.

Yet, even as they discussed the progress of the construction and the vision for the grand house in

Notting Hill, the echoes of their earlier conversation lingered in the background, a silent reminder of the deeper currents that flowed beneath the surface of their professional collaboration.

The Thorntons, driven by a desire to expedite the completion of the refurbishment, urged them to cut the timeline in half, aiming to finish the project within just two months.

Richard and James exchanged incredulous glances, the weight of the new deadline settling heavily upon them. The challenge ahead seemed daunting, yet they were determined to rise to the occasion and meet the Thorntons' ambitious expectations.

With renewed resolve, they devised a plan to streamline their efforts and maximise efficiency, knowing that the project's success hinged upon their ability to deliver within the tightened timeframe.

Feeling the weight of their ongoing challenges and the need for additional support on the project, the Thornton family suggested hiring a new team member to accelerate the project's completion. They recommended David, having reviewed his impressive portfolio and recognised his expertise and experience in similar refurbishments.

Richard and James exchanged thoughtful glances, considering the practicality of the Thorntons' suggestion. Recognising the potential benefits of having an experienced ally join their team, they agreed to bring David on board, welcoming him into their collaborative effort to bring the grand house in Notting Hill to fruition.

David was brought on board to ease the weight of ongoing challenges and enhance the team's project support. With a sense of optimism about the additional support David would bring, Richard and James set their sights on the next phase of the construction project, eager to harness their team's collective expertise and dedication as they navigated the challenges ahead.

David, a Londoner in his early thirties, exudes a distinctively British charm with his tousled blond hair, intense blue eyes, and features that reflect determination and resilience. He lives in Soho, where his apartment is a reflection of his eclectic tastes and artistic sensibilities. David's human side was further revealed through his bond with his feline companion, Lissa. Adopted from a local shelter, Lissa was more than just a pet to David; she was his faithful confidante, providing comfort and companionship after long days on the construction site. David often joked that Lissa ruled the roost in his apartment, with her playful antics bringing joy and warmth to his life.

In addition to his beloved cat, David had a surprising passion for orchids. Despite his rugged exterior, he found solace in caring for these delicate flowers; each blooms a testament to his patience and dedication. His apartment was adorned with pots of orchids in various colours and varieties, their beauty bringing a touch of tranquillity to his home.

These glimpses into David's personal life humanised him in the eyes of those around him, revealing a softer, more nurturing side to his personality. His bond with Lissa and his appreciation for the beauty of orchids added depth to his character, highlighting the multifaceted nature of his identity beyond his role as a construction worker.

During the first week on the construction site, Richard, James, and David dove headfirst into their tasks, each bringing their unique skills and expertise to the project.

Richard, with his architectural vision and attention to detail, oversaw the overall design and layout of the house, meticulously planning every aspect of the refurbishment.

James, with his hands-on experience and practical know-how, led the construction efforts, coordinating with subcontractors and ensuring that the work progressed smoothly.

Meanwhile, David, with his strength and agility, tackled the physical labour, hauling materials and assisting with the more labour-intensive tasks.

Despite the challenges inherent in any construction project, the three men worked seamlessly together, their strengths complementing one another as they tackled each new challenge that arose. From laying the foundation to installing the framework, they made steady progress, fuelled by a shared sense of purpose and camaraderie.

As they toiled under the sun, their banter filled the air, punctuated by laughter and occasional teasing. They shared stories from their past, swapped jokes, and bonded over shared experiences, forging a sense of camaraderie that would become the foundation of their working relationship.

Despite the long hours and physical exertion, seeing their progress take shape gave them a sense of satisfaction. With each passing day, the once-dilapidated house began to transform into a modern masterpiece, a testament to their hard work and dedication.

As the sun dipped below the horizon on the final day of the week, Richard, James, and David stood side by side, surveying their handiwork with pride. Though there was still much work to be done, they couldn't help but feel a sense of accomplishment at how far they had come in just one short week. And with renewed determination, they set their sights on the challenges ahead, ready to tackle them together as a team.

During the second week on the construction site, Richard, James, and David continued to make significant progress on the refurbishment project. With the foundation laid and the framework in place, they shifted their focus to the finer details of the renovation, each task bringing them closer to their goal of completing the project on time.

Richard delved deeper into the architectural aspects of the project, fine-tuning the design elements and making adjustments as needed to ensure that every aspect of the house met his exacting standards. His keen eye for detail and unwavering commitment to excellence drove him to push the boundaries of creativity, exploring innovative solutions to enhance the space's functionality and aesthetic appeal.

Meanwhile, James led the construction efforts with unwavering determination, overseeing the work of the subcontractors and ensuring that each phase of the project was executed with precision and care. His hands-on approach and practical expertise proved invaluable as he navigated the complexities of the construction process, troubleshooting issues and finding solutions to any challenges.

David, ever reliable and hardworking, continued to lend his strength and skill to the physical labour involved in the project. From hauling materials to assisting with the installation of fixtures and fittings, he approached each task with a tireless work ethic and a willingness to go above and beyond to get the job done.

As the days passed, their teamwork and collaboration became even more
seamless, their roles merging into a cohesive unit working towards a common goal. Despite the inevitable setbacks and obstacles they encountered, their determination never wavered, fuelled by a shared sense of purpose and mutual respect's abilities.

By the end of the second week, significant progress had been made, and the once dilapidated house was beginning to take on a new life. With each passing day, Richard, James, and David grew more confident in their abilities and more determined than ever to see the project through to completion. Looking ahead to the coming weeks, they knew that anything was possible with hard work, dedication, and teamwork.

The morning sun filtered through the grand bay windows of the historic Notting Hill house, casting intricate patterns on the wooden floors. The scent of fresh paint and the faint buzz of power tools filled the air, blending with the distant hum of London outside. Richard Cutler stood at the centre of the drawing room, studying the detailed blueprints spread out on an antique oak table. The room, like the house, was a blend of history and potential, much like the lives of those working within it.

On that morning, the delivery company arrived with a shipment of materials for the refurbishment project. David was assigned to oversee the delivery, ensuring that everything matched the order and inspecting the inventory with a practiced eye. As he meticulously checked the items, one particular individual among the delivery crew caught his attention. There was something unsettling about the man—a familiarity that sent a shiver down David's spine.

Despite the wave of unease that washed over him, David maintained his composure, completing his task with efficiency and professionalism. Once the delivery was confirmed and the paperwork finalised, he made his way to the room where Richard was working, trying to shake off the lingering sense of dread.

James Turner entered, wiping his hands on a cloth. His eyes were distant, as though he was contemplating more than just the work ahead. Richard noticed this and raised an eyebrow.

"Everything alright, James?" Richard asked, folding the blueprints neatly.
James hesitated, then nodded. "Yeah, just... thinking about some things." He forced a smile, but it didn't reach his eyes.

Richard decided not to press further, knowing that James would speak when he was ready. They worked in companionable silence for a while, the only sounds being the rhythmic tap of hammers and the occasional murmur of conversation from other workers. As the morning wore on, Richard saw the tension lines in James's face deepening.

"Let's take a break," Richard suggested. "Coffee?"

James nodded gratefully, and they made their way to a makeshift kitchenette in the corner of the house. They poured two steaming mugs and settled onto a pair of sturdy stools. Richard waited patiently, sensing that James had something weighing heavily on his mind.

After a few sips, James finally spoke, his voice quiet. "You ever have something from your past that you can't seem to shake off, no matter how hard you try?"

Richard considered the question. "We all have our ghosts, I suppose. Why do you ask?"

James stared into his coffee as if it held the answers he sought. "When I was sixteen, I had an affair. With an older man."

The confession hung in the air between them, heavy and unexpected. Richard remained silent, giving James the space to continue.

"His name was Mark. He was a friend of the family, someone I looked up to. It started innocently enough, but... it became more." James's voice trembled slightly. "I was just a kid but thought I was in love. He made me feel special, important."

Richard listened, understanding that James had carried this alone for a long time.

"It ended abruptly," James continued. "He moved away and left without a word. I was devastated. It was like losing a part of myself. I never told anyone, not even Emily. I've buried it for years, but being back in London, with all its memories and possibilities, has brought it all back."

Richard reached out, placing a reassuring hand on James's shoulder. "Thank you for sharing that, James. It sounds like it was a difficult time. Have you ever thought about talking to someone, a professional, maybe?"

James shook his head. "I wouldn't know where to start. But being here, working on this house, it's like I'm finally confronting parts of myself I've kept hidden. It's scary, but maybe it's time."

Richard nodded. "Sometimes, facing the past is the only way to move forward. And you're not alone in this. We're a team, remember?"

James smiled a genuine one this time. "Thanks, Richard. I appreciate it."

Their break over, they returned to their work with renewed determination. As James chipped away at the old plaster, revealing the layers of history beneath, he felt a strange sense of liberation. Each stroke of the hammer, each brush of paint, was like peeling back the layers of his past, bringing buried truths into the light.

The revelation of James's teenage affair added a new layer to their project, intertwining personal history with the physical restoration of the house. The lines between past and present blurred as they worked, creating a tapestry of experiences that shaped their identities and journeys together.

In the days that followed, James found himself opening up more, not just to Richard but also to David. The house, with its secrets and stories, became a place of healing and discovery. And as they uncovered its hidden past, they also began to find their own, forging a deeper bond and understanding along the way.

For weeks, James had been wrestling with the state of his marriage to his wife, Emily. What had once been a union filled with love and laughter had gradually soured, poisoned by resentment and misunderstandings. Their once-strong bond had frayed, worn thin by the strain of conflicting priorities and unspoken grievances.

Despite his best efforts to salvage their relationship, James found himself at a crossroads, torn between his desire to make things work and the painful realisation that, sometimes, love wasn't enough. The rift between them had grown too deep to bridge, the chasm widening with each passing day.

And so, with a heavy heart and a sense of resignation, James made the difficult decision to end his marriage. It was a choice fraught with uncertainty and heartache, but deep down, he knew it was the right thing to do. For both his sake and Emily's, it was time to let go and move on, to seek out a new beginning untethered by the weight of the past.

As he faced the prospect of starting anew, James found solace in the camaraderie of his colleagues on the construction site. Richard and David became his confidants, offering support and understanding as he navigated the turbulent waters of his personal life. Their unwavering friendship provided a beacon of hope amid the darkness, reminding him that he was not alone in his struggles.

And so, with a heavy heart and a sense of determination, James took the first step towards a brighter future, knowing that though the road ahead would be fraught with challenges, he would face them with courage and resilience, fortified by the bonds of friendship that had become his lifeline in times of need.

The next weeks, however, turned his life into a living hell. What he had hoped to resolve calmly and amicably escalated into a relentless storm of conflict and emotional turmoil.

Emily's behaviour grew increasingly erratic and vindictive, her manipulation and hostility intensifying. She fought him at every turn, using their daughter as leverage and spreading lies that painted James as the villain in their fractured marriage.

The arguments became a battleground, with James fighting desperately to maintain his sense of self-worth in the face of Emily's relentless attacks. He tried to reason with her, to appeal to her sense of reason and empathy, but his efforts were met with hostility and indifference.

Caught in the crossfire were their daughter, who bore witness to the escalating tension between their parents. James watched helplessly as Emily's behaviour took its toll on their impressionable minds, her narcissistic tendencies leaving scars that ran deep.

Despite his best efforts to shield them from harm, James couldn't protect his daughter from the emotional turmoil surrounding them. He watched with a heavy heart as they struggled to make sense of the chaos unfolding before their eyes, their innocence slowly eroded by the toxicity of their parent's relationship.

Amid the chaos, James grappled with a sense of powerlessness, his frustration boiling over into anger and resentment. He longed for a sense of peace and stability, a refuge from the storm that raged within the walls of his own home.

And so, with a heavy heart and a sense of resignation, James made the difficult decision to confront Emily head-on, to stand up for himself and his daughter in the face of her tyranny. It was a battle he knew he couldn't win alone, but he was determined to fight nonetheless, fuelled by a fierce determination to reclaim his dignity and self-worth.

As James confronted Emily's narcissistic control and harassment, the tension in their home reached a boiling point. Emily's behaviour became increasingly unpredictable and volatile; her need for dominance drove her to lash out with increasing frequency and intensity.

Her words cut like knives, slicing through James' defences and leaving him emotionally battered and bruised. She manipulated their daughter, using them as leverage to maintain her hold over

James, and he watched helplessly as they became unwitting participants in her toxic games.

The once-loving home they had built together became a battleground, each interaction tinged with hostility and resentment. James felt like he was walking on eggshells, never knowing when the next explosion would occur or what would set it off.

Despite his efforts to reason with her and find common ground, Emily remained obstinate and unyielding. Her need for control drove a wedge between them that seemed impossible to bridge. James felt suffocated by her presence, and his attempts to assert himself were met with resistance at every turn.

During the chaos, James struggled to maintain his sense of self, his confidence eroded by Emily's constant criticism and manipulation. He felt like he was losing himself, his identity slipping away beneath the weight of her relentless onslaught.

But amidst the darkness, there was a glimmer of hope—a spark of defiance that flickered to life within James' heart. He refused to be broken by

Emily's tyranny, determined to reclaim his sense of autonomy and forge a path forward, free from the chains of her control.

And so, with a heavy heart and a sense of resolve, James made the difficult decision to confront Emily and put an end to the cycle of abuse. It was a decision that would change their lives forever, but he knew it was necessary for his sanity and well-being.

Feeling emotionally drained and overwhelmed by the turmoil in his personal life, James made the difficult decision to take a temporary break from the chaos at home and focus on the construction site. It was a choice born out of necessity, a lifeline he desperately clung to in the storm raging within him.

As he stepped onto the familiar grounds of the construction site, James felt a sense of relief wash over him. Here, amidst the hustle and bustle of the workday, he found solace in the rhythmic pounding of hammers and the drone of machinery. It was a welcome distraction from the turmoil brewing in his personal life, a reprieve from the chaos that threatened to consume him.

At the construction site, the support of Richard and David became his only refuge. Their friendship and understanding offered a brief respite from the chaos, allowing him to focus on the project and find moments of peace amidst the turmoil. Yet, even their unwavering support couldn't completely shield him from the relentless stress that followed him everywhere.

Together, they tackled the challenges of the construction site as a united front, their camaraderie providing a sense of stability and purpose amidst the uncertainty of James' personal life. With each passing day, James felt a renewed sense of strength and resilience, fortified by the bonds of friendship that sustained him.

As he immersed himself in the tasks, James found peace amidst the chaos, a fleeting moment of respite from the storm that raged within him. Here, amidst the construction site, he found a sense of purpose and belonging, a sanctuary where he could set aside his worries and focus on the task.

But even as he threw himself into his work, James knew that the challenges awaiting him at home would not disappear overnight. The road ahead would be long and arduous, filled with obstacles and setbacks. Yet, with the support of his colleagues by his side, he felt a glimmer of hope that he could weather the storm and emerge stronger on the other side.

Amid his frustration and emotional turmoil, James was drawn to David in a way he hadn't anticipated. Their shared experiences on the construction site had forged a bond between them, a connection that went beyond mere camaraderie.

CHAPTER 6

JAMES'S SECRET AFFAIR

One evening, David invited Richard and James to join him for a quiz pub night at a lively spot in Notting Hill, just a stone's throw from the construction site where they had been working. It was a welcome break after the relentless grind of the job, and a chance to unwind and have some fun.

The pub was bustling with energy as teams competed for the top prize, and the atmosphere was filled with laughter and camaraderie. David, ever the gracious host, was excited to share the evening with his friends. James and Richard, eager to escape their daily stresses, eagerly accepted the invitation.

As the night progressed, the trio found themselves deeply engrossed in the quiz. David's knowledge of obscure trivia proved invaluable, while James and Richard's teamwork added a spirited edge to their performance. They tackled questions on a range of topics, from history to pop culture, with varying degrees of success. Their banter and shared enthusiasm for the game made for a lively and enjoyable experience.

The pints flowed freely as the night wore on. They raised their glasses to celebrate their successes and commiserate over their missed answers. The pub's warm, inviting atmosphere and the clinking of glasses created a backdrop for their growing friendship and sense of camaraderie.

As the pub began to wind down for the night and the staff started to clean up, David saw an opportunity for the evening to continue. He turned to James with a grin and extended an invitation. "Hey, how about we head to my place for a nightcap? I've got some great drinks at home, and we can keep the fun going."

Richard, who had a tight schedule due to a visit to his family in Bath the following day, decided it was time to say his goodbyes. He bid his friends farewell, his departure marked by a round of hearty goodbyes and promises to catch up soon.

With Richard off to bed early, David and James took the short walk to David's home, their spirits high and their conversation flowing. The promise of more drinks and relaxed company made the transition from the pub to David's home feel like a natural extension of their evening.

As they settled in at David's place, the atmosphere was warm and inviting, a perfect continuation of their night out. They enjoyed a selection of drinks and delved into deeper conversations, their laughter and camaraderie undiminished by the change in venue.

For a few hours, the pressures and issues of the construction site were left behind. The night was a testament to their bond, a reminder of the simple joys of friendship and shared experiences. As the evening drew to a close, both James and David felt a sense of contentment, grateful for the respite and connection they had enjoyed.

Little did they know, the evening would be more than just a pleasant distraction—it would set the stage for the deepening of their relationship, a connection that would soon surpass the boundaries of mere friendship.

As David and James settled into the cozy ambiance of David's home, the evening took on a more intimate tone. The drinks were flowing, their laughter echoing warmly in the small but inviting space. David's gentle demeanour and compassionate nature created an atmosphere of comfort and safety that allowed James to relax and open up in ways he hadn't before.

James was immediately taken by the charm of David's house. It had a unique character that he found both intriguing and comforting. The living room was filled with an array of lush plants that added a touch of nature and tranquility to the space. A soft, warm light illuminated the room, creating an inviting atmosphere. James noticed the cat, Lissa, a playful and affectionate feline who seemed to take an immediate liking to him.

As David went to the kitchen to prepare more drinks, James stayed behind, captivated by Lissa's playful antics. He found himself lost in the simple joy of playing with the cat, the softness of her fur and her curious, endearing behaviour providing a welcome distraction.

Their conversations flowed effortlessly, ranging from personal struggles to shared dreams. The more they talked, the more James felt a deep sense of solace in David's presence, as if he had finally found someone who truly understood him. They found refuge in each other's company, a welcome escape from the chaos and uncertainties that had been plaguing their lives.

As the night progressed, the initial spark of their friendship began to ignite into something more profound. Their connection deepened with each shared glance and casual touch. It was clear that their feelings were evolving, moving beyond mere camaraderie.

David, sensing the shifting dynamic between them, decided it was time to address the growing attraction head-on. As they sat close together on the couch, the warm glow of the lamp casting a soft light over their faces, David took a deep breath.

"James," he began, his voice steady but filled with an emotional undercurrent, "there's something I need to tell you." He looked into James's eyes, searching for a reaction. "I've felt a strong physical attraction to you for a while now. It's more than just the friendship we've built—it's something deeper."

James met David's gaze, his heart pounding as the weight of David's words settled in. He had felt the shift too, the subtle but undeniable pull between them. The tension in the air was thick with unspoken desire.

David's confession was both a relief and a challenge. It was a moment of vulnerability, where he laid bare his feelings and exposed the depth of his attraction. James, taken aback but intrigued, responded with a quiet nod, acknowledging the truth in David's words.

Their emotions, long simmering beneath the surface, surged forth with a new intensity. The gentle touches that had been fleeting and innocent now took on a more charged significance. It wasn't long before David's hand found James's, their fingers intertwining in a gesture that spoke of shared longing and unspoken promises.

As the night wore on, their physical attraction became impossible to ignore. The small touches turned into lingering caresses, and the stolen glances became full, unguarded looks of desire. In a moment of raw emotion and mutual understanding, they allowed themselves to be drawn into each other's arms.

Their embrace was tender but passionate, a collision of bodies and souls that left them both breathless. It was a desperate attempt to find solace and connection amid the tumult of their emotions. In the aftermath of their encounter, as they lay tangled together, they both felt a profound sense of release—a temporary escape from the turmoil that had consumed them.

But as they lay together, basking in the warmth and intimacy they had shared, James couldn't help but reflect on the significance of what had just happened. Their connection went beyond mere physical attraction; it was a profound emotional bond that transcended words and gestures. In David's arms, James found a sanctuary from the chaos of his life, a place where he could let down his guard and simply be.

As they drifted off to sleep, entwined in each other's embrace, James felt a mixture of peace and apprehension. He knew that their newfound closeness was more than just a fleeting escape—it was a significant shift in their relationship that would have far-reaching consequences.

The comfort of David's presence was a balm for James's troubled soul, but it also came with a swirl of conflicting emotions. The thought of Richard and the weight of his commitments to his wife and family loomed large in his mind. He was torn between the comfort of familiarity and the allure of the unknown, acutely aware of the challenges and sacrifices that lay ahead.

As he lay awake in the darkness, James grappled with the weight of his choices, knowing that the road forward would be fraught with difficulties.

The threshold he had crossed was one from which there was no return, and the only thing left was to face the consequences of his actions with courage and conviction.

The next morning, as they lounged in the light of the late summer sun streaming through the windows, James felt a renewed sense of clarity and affection. Their night together had opened a new chapter in their relationship, and James found himself eager to extend the connection they had established.

As they sipped their coffee and talked about their plans, James decided to seize the moment. "You know," he began, his voice carrying a hint of both excitement and nervousness, "with Richard away in Bath this weekend, it seems like a great opportunity for us to spend more time together. How about you come over to my place for the weekend? I'd love to have you as my guest."

David looked at James with a mix of surprise and delight. The invitation was both a continuation of their recent intimacy and an opportunity to explore their connection further. "That sounds wonderful," David replied, a smile spreading across his face. "I'd really like that."

The weekend at David's house was filled with warmth and discovery. The space was cozy and welcoming, with its lush plants and charming decor creating a soothing atmosphere.

They enjoyed leisurely mornings, shared meals, and the comfort of each other's company. Their time together solidified the bond they had started to build, and each moment felt like a step towards something more profound.

However, as Sunday evening approached, James became mindful of the practicalities of their situation. Richard was scheduled to return from Bath the next day, and James knew he needed to be back at the Notting Hill house before Richard's arrival. With a sense of mixed emotions, he discussed the plan with David.

"I think it's time for me to head back to Notting Hill," James said as they wrapped up their final evening together. "Richard will be back tomorrow, and I need to be there before he returns. I want to make sure everything is as it should be."

David nodded, understanding the need for James to return to his home. "I get it," he said. "I've really enjoyed our time together this weekend. It's been special."

As they said their goodbyes, there was a bittersweet quality to the moment. The weekend had been a revelation, and the connection they had forged was something James deeply valued.

With a promise to stay in touch and an unspoken agreement to navigate the future together, James left for Notting Hill, carrying with him the memory of their time together and the anticipation of what might come next.

As James returned to the construction site, his mind was filled with a whirlwind of conflicting emotions.

When Richard finally walked through the door, James was waiting in the hallway. He approached him with a forced smile that didn't quite reach his eyes. "Welcome back, Richard," James said, trying to sound casual.

Richard, carrying the easy confidence of someone refreshed by a family visit, smiled warmly in return. "Thanks, James. It's good to be back. How was the weekend here?"

James's mind raced, struggling to maintain a semblance of normalcy. "Oh, it was fine. Just the usual routine," he replied, his voice betraying a hint of tension.

Despite his attempts to project calm, James couldn't shake the feeling of unease that gnawed at him from within. Every gesture, every word exchanged with Richard felt like a reminder of the secret he was keeping—a secret that now seemed to hover in the air between them.

Richard, ever perceptive, noticed the tension in James' demeanour and inquired if everything was alright. James hesitated momentarily, grappling with the internal turmoil that threatened to consume him. How could he explain what had transpired between him and David without betraying the trust of his friend and colleague?

Forced to confront the reality of his actions, James faltered, his words catching in his throat. He mumbled something about a restless night and quickly changed the subject, deflecting Richard's inquiries with practised ease.

But even as he went about his duties on the construction site, James couldn't shake the guilt and confusion that weighed heavily upon him. What had happened between him and David stirred something deep within him, a longing and desire he couldn't easily dismiss.

As the new day dawned, the house at Notting Hill seemed to be slowly returning to its usual rhythm. However, James found it difficult to shake off the turbulent emotions that had been swirling within him since Richard's return.

Caught between his feelings for David and his loyalty to Richard, James grappled with the impossible choice that lay before him. And as he navigated the complexities of his emotions, he knew that the road ahead would be fraught with challenges and uncertainty. But for now, all he could do was bury his feelings deep within and focus on the task at hand, hoping against hope that he could find a way to reconcile the conflicting desires that raged within him.

Throughout the day, James tried to maintain a facade of normalcy, burying his inner turmoil beneath a mask of professionalism. Yet, with each passing moment, the memory of his intimate encounter with David lingered like a persistent shadow, refusing to be ignored.

As the sun began to dip below the horizon and the day drew to a close, James found himself unable to shake the weight of his conflicted emotions. He stole furtive glances in David's direction, his heart aching with longing and regret.

Richard, ever observant, sensed that something was amiss, but James brushed off his concerns with practised ease. He couldn't bear to burden his colleague with the weight of his turmoil, not when he was still grappling with the enormity of what had transpired.

And so, as the final moments of daylight slipped away, James made a silent vow to confront his feelings head-on, to navigate the treacherous waters of desire and loyalty with courage and integrity. He knew that the road ahead would be fraught with challenges and uncertainty, but he was determined to face it with unwavering resolve.

As he bid farewell to Richard and David, James felt a sense of determination wash over him. Whatever the future held, he knew that he couldn't continue to deny the truth of his desires. And with that newfound clarity, he set out into the night, ready to confront the tangled web of emotions that threatened to consume him.

James hesitated for a moment, torn between the desire to spend more time with David and the nagging sense of guilt that gnawed at his conscience. The memory of their intimate encounter still lingered fresh in his mind, casting a shadow over his every thought.

But despite his reservations, James found himself unable to resist the pull of David's invitation. There was something about the other man's presence that drew him in, a magnetic force that he couldn't quite explain.

With a sense of trepidation mingled with anticipation, James accepted David's invitation, his heart pounding with a mixture of excitement and uncertainty. He knew that this decision would only complicate matters further, but at that moment, all he could focus on was the promise of escape, of finding solace in David's company once more.

And so, as the evening descended into the night and the city lights twinkled in the distance, James found himself standing outside David's door, his pulse racing with anticipation. With a steadying breath, he raised his hand to knock, ready to confront the whirlwind of emotions that awaited him on the other side.

In the weeks that followed, James found himself increasingly drawn to David's company. They spent evenings together, sharing drinks and engaging in deep, meaningful conversations that delved into the depths of their souls. With each passing day, James felt himself opening up to David in ways he never thought possible, sharing his fears, hopes, and dreams with a vulnerability he had long kept hidden.

As their bond deepened, James couldn't help but feel a growing sense of guilt for betraying Richard's trust. He knew that he was treading dangerous waters, risking not only his friendship with Richard but also the stability of his marriage. Yet, despite his best efforts to resist, he found himself inexorably drawn to David, unable to deny the magnetic pull of their connection.

Meanwhile, Richard remained oblivious to the turmoil brewing beneath the surface. He threw himself into his work, channelling his energy into the construction project with a single-minded focus that left little room for introspection. Yet, despite his outward facade of confidence, Richard couldn't shake the nagging sense that something was amiss, a lingering suspicion that whispered secrets hidden just out of sight.

As the days turned into weeks, the tension between James and Richard began to simmer beneath the surface, threatening to boil over at any moment. Yet, neither man dared to confront the truth of their feelings, choosing instead to bury their desires deep within, where they lay dormant, waiting to be unleashed.

And so, as they navigated the complexities of their relationships, James and Richard found themselves teetering on the edge of a precipice, unsure of what the future held. Caught between loyalty and desire, duty and passion, they stood at a crossroads, their fates intertwined in ways they could never have imagined.

As they toiled away on the construction site, the rhythmic sound of hammers and saws filling the air, Richard couldn't shake the feeling of unease that had been gnawing at him for weeks. He had noticed the subtle shifts in James' demeanour, the lingering glances exchanged between him and David, and he couldn't ignore the growing sense of tension that seemed to hover between them like a heavy cloud.

Unable to contain his curiosity any longer, Richard finally broached the subject, his voice tinged with concern as he turned to James. "Hey, James," he began tentatively, "I've been meaning to ask... what's been going on between you and David lately?

James froze for a moment, his heart pounding in his chest as he searched for the right words to respond. He knew that he couldn't continue to hide the truth from Richard, yet the thought of confessing his feelings filled him with a sense of dread.

Taking a deep breath, James met Richard's gaze with a mixture of apprehension and resignation. "It's complicated," he admitted, his voice barely above a whisper. "I... I don't know how to explain it."

Richard studied James for a moment, his brow furrowing in concern as he sensed the weight of his friend's words. "Whatever it is, James, you can talk to me about it," he offered gently. "I'm here for you, no matter what."

James felt a surge of gratitude wash over him at Richard's words, a flicker of hope amidst the turmoil raging within him. "Thanks, Richard," he murmured, his voice thick with emotion. "I... I'll tell you everything, I promise. But right now, I need some time to figure things out."

With that, James turned away, his thoughts consumed by the tangled web of emotions that threatened to engulf him. As he continued to work alongside Richard, he couldn't shake the feeling that the truth was slowly unravelling, inch by inch, bringing him ever closer to a reckoning he could no longer avoid.

As the sun beat down upon the construction site, Richard's inquiry hung heavy in the air, casting a palpable tension over the scene. James felt a knot form in his stomach as he grappled with the weight of Richard's question, the words echoing in his mind like a relentless drumbeat.

Sweat beaded on James' brow as he struggled to find the right words, his thoughts racing a mile a minute. He knew that he couldn't keep hiding the truth from Richard, yet the prospect of revealing his inner turmoil filled him with a sense of dread.

Finally, after what felt like an eternity of silence, James summoned the courage to respond. "It's... complicated," he began, his voice wavering slightly. "David and I... we've been spending much time together, and... things have gotten... complicated."

Richard's brow furrowed in concern as he listened to James' halting words, a mixture of confusion and apprehension clouding his features.

"Complicated how?" he pressed gently, his eyes searching James' face for answers.

James hesitated for a moment, grappling with how much to reveal. He knew that he couldn't keep Richard in the dark any longer, yet the fear of judgment weighed heavily on his mind.
Taking a deep breath, James forged ahead, his voice tinged with uncertainty. "I... I think I have feelings for David," he admitted quietly, his words hanging in the air like a heavy fog.

Richard's eyes widened in surprise at James' confession, his mind reeling with the implications of his friend's words. He had never considered the possibility that James might harbour romantic feelings for another man, and the revelation left him struggling to process the enormity of what he had just heard.

For a long moment, silence descended upon the construction site, broken only by the distant hum of machinery and the soft rustle of the breeze. Richard searched for the right words to say, his mind racing as he grappled with the weight of James' confession.

Finally, he reached out a hand and gently placed it on James' shoulder, offering a silent gesture of support. "James," he said softly, his voice filled with empathy, "I may not understand everything you're going through right now, but I want you to know I'm here for you. Whatever you need, I'll be here to support you every step of the way."

James felt a surge of gratitude wash over him at Richard's words, a sense of relief flooding his senses as he realised that he didn't have to face his struggles alone. At that moment, he knew that no matter what the future held, he had a friend who would stand by him through thick and thin.

As James grappled with the complexities of his burgeoning feelings for David, he couldn't shake the weight of societal preconceptions that loomed over him like a dark cloud. Growing up in a world where heteronormativity reigned supreme, James had internalised the idea that love and relationships were reserved solely for those who fit neatly into society's predetermined moulds.

The mere thought of deviating from these norms filled James with a sense of unease, a fear of being judged and ostracised by those around him. He had spent years hiding his true self, burying his desires beneath layers of denial and repression in a desperate bid to conform to society's expectations.

But now, as he found himself falling for David, James couldn't ignore the nagging voice in the back of his mind that whispered of the dangers that awaited him should he dare to embrace his truth. The fear of rejection, of being labelled as "other" or "different," gnawed at his insides, threatening to suffocate him beneath its suffocating weight.

And yet, despite the overwhelming apprehension that threatened to consume him, James couldn't deny his undeniable pull towards David. Their connection transcended the boundaries of societal norms, existing in a realm where love knew no bounds and authenticity reigned supreme.

But as James grappled with the complexities of his feelings, he couldn't shake the nagging sense of doubt that lingered in the depths of his soul. What would his family and friends think if they knew the truth? Would they accept him for who he truly was, or would they turn their backs on him in disgust?

These questions weighed heavily on James' mind as he navigated the treacherous waters of his burgeoning relationship with David. He knew that the road ahead would be fraught with challenges and obstacles, but he also knew that he couldn't deny the truth of his heart any longer.

With each passing day, James grew more determined to defy the expectations that had long held him captive, break free from societal oppression, and embrace the love that had blossomed between him
and David. As he embarked on this journey of self-discovery and acceptance, James knew he would stop at nothing to carve out a space for himself in a world that too often sought to erase his existence.

As Richard processed James' revelation about his feelings for David, he grappled with a whirlwind of emotions and thoughts. Raised in a society where traditional notions of love and relationships were deeply ingrained, Richard couldn't help but feel a twinge of discomfort at the prospect of his friend embarking on a same-sex relationship.

However, as he reflected on James and David's connection, Richard realised that his initial discomfort stemmed more from societal conditioning than genuine concern for his friend's happiness. He recognised that love knew no bounds and that James and David's relationship was no less valid or meaningful simply because it defied conventional norms.

With this realisation came a newfound sense of empathy and understanding. Richard knew that James had struggled for years to come to terms with his identity, and he couldn't help but admire his friend's courage in embracing his truth despite the challenges he faced.

Armed with this perspective, Richard resolved to be a source of support and guidance for James as he navigated the complexities of his budding relationship with David. He knew that his friend would need someone to lean on during this tumultuous time, and he was determined to be there for him every step of the way.

In the days and weeks that followed, Richard offered James a listening ear and a shoulder to lean on whenever he needed it. He encouraged his friend to embrace his feelings for David and to follow his heart, regardless of what others might think.

At the same time, Richard doesn't hesitate to offer his advice and perspective when James faces challenges or doubts along the way. He reminded his friend that love was worth fighting for and that true happiness could only be found by staying true to oneself, no matter the obstacles that stood in the way.

As James continued navigating the ups and downs of his relationship with David, Richard remained steadfast in his life, offering unwavering support and encouragement every step of the way. In doing so, he not only helped his friend find the courage to embrace his truth but also deepened his understanding of love, acceptance, and the true meaning of friendship.

Ever the voice of reason and pragmatism, Richard pulled James and David aside one day as they worked together on the construction site. With a stern yet compassionate expression, he urged them to exercise discretion and respect in their budding relationship.

"I want you both to know that I fully support you," Richard began, his tone firm yet empathetic. "But we need to be mindful of our surroundings on the construction site. Not everyone may be as accepting as I am, and we must maintain a professional demeanour while working."

He paused, his gaze shifting between James and David, both of whom nodded in understanding.

"I trust you both will be respectful and discreet," Richard continued. "Affection should be kept private between the two of you. This isn't about hiding who you are—it's about being mindful of our environment and the potential consequences of openly displaying your relationship."

James and David exchanged a knowing glance, silently acknowledging Richard's wisdom. They understood the importance of discretion, especially in a setting where their relationship might not be universally accepted.

"Thank you, Richard," James said, his voice filled with gratitude. "We appreciate your support and your guidance. We'll make sure to keep things professional and respectful."

With that, they returned to their work, a newfound sense of determination and purpose guiding their actions. As they continued to navigate the complexities of their relationship, they did so with Richard's words of wisdom echoing in their minds, a reminder of the importance of discretion and respect in their journey forward.

As James became increasingly drawn to David, he couldn't shake the feeling that their connection went beyond mere camaraderie. The more time they spent together on the construction site, the stronger his feelings grew until he could no longer deny the truth that lay at the core of his being.

But as James grappled with the realisation that he was falling for David, he couldn't shake the nagging sense of apprehension that gnawed at his insides. What if David didn't feel the same way? What if their relationship jeopardised their friendship and the camaraderie they had built on the construction site?

These questions swirled in James' mind as he mulled over his next move. Eventually, he decided to confront his feelings head-on, lay bare the truth of his heart, and see where it led.

With trembling hands and a racing heart, James approached David one afternoon after work and bared his soul, confessing his feelings and the longing that had taken root in his heart. To his relief, David's response
was one of understanding and acceptance, as he confessed to harbouring feelings for James.

At that moment, a weight lifted off James' shoulders, replaced by a sense of relief and euphoria unlike anything he had ever experienced before. With David by his side, he felt a sense of completeness and belonging that he had never known, a feeling that washed over him like a warm embrace.

As they navigated the uncharted waters of their budding relationship, James found himself growing closer to David with each passing day.

They spent long hours talking and laughing together, sharing their hopes, dreams, and fears as they explored the depths of their newfound connection.

Eventually, James decided to move out from the construction site and into David's house, eager to take their relationship to the next level and see where it led. As he settled into his new home with David by his side, James knew he had finally found the love and acceptance he had been searching for all along.

Richard arranged to travel to Bath for the weekend to spend time with his family. It was a welcomed chance for him to escape the urban hustle of London and reconnect with his roots in the serene surroundings of Bath.

Richard sat across from his wife, Sarah, feeling the weight of his revelation pressing down on him. He cleared his throat, gathering his thoughts before speaking.

"Sarah, there's something I need to discuss with you," he began, his voice steady but tinged with apprehension.

Sarah looked up from her book, her gaze meeting Richard's with a mixture of curiosity and concern. "What is it, Richard? Is everything okay?"

Richard took a deep breath, trying to find the right words to convey the situation's complexity. "It's about James and David," he started, his words carefully measured.

Sarah's brow furrowed in confusion. "James and David? What about them?"

Richard hesitated, knowing that his following words would come as a shock. "They're in a relationship," he admitted, watching for Sarah's reaction.

Sarah's eyes widened in surprise, her mouth falling open slightly. "What? But... how?" she stammered, clearly shocked by the news.

Richard nodded, his heart heavy with the weight of the revelation. "I'm not entirely sure, but... they're together," he confirmed.

Sarah took a moment to process the information, her expression shifting from surprise to concern.

"But James is married, isn't he?" she asked, her voice tinged with worry.

Richard nodded gravely. "Yes, he is. And that's part of what makes this so complicated," he explained. "But they care about each other, Sarah. They're in love."

Sarah's features softened with understanding, though she still looked troubled. "I see," she said quietly. "That must be incredibly difficult for James, especially with his family."

Richard nodded in agreement. "It is," he admitted. "And that's why I wanted to talk to you about it. I want to support James, but I'm not sure how."

Sarah reached out, placing a comforting hand on Richard's arm. "We'll figure it out together," she reassured him. "The most important thing is to be there for him, no matter what."

Richard felt a surge of gratitude for Sarah's understanding and support. "Thank you, Sarah," he said sincerely. "I'm glad we could talk about this."

As they sat together in silence, Richard felt a sense of relief wash over him. Despite the challenges ahead, he knew that he and Sarah would face them together, united in their commitment to supporting their friend in his time of need.

As the weekend came to a close, Richard felt a sense of renewal and determination. He knew that returning to London would mean confronting the challenges ahead, but he also found comfort in knowing that James and David were there for each other, no matter the distance. With his family's support behind him, Richard was ready to face whatever the future held, knowing that love and understanding would guide them through the journey ahead.

As they sat in silence, Richard's mind churned with thoughts of navigating the complexities of James and David's relationship. He knew that supporting James would require delicacy and understanding, but he also grappled with his own emotions about the situation.

After a moment, Sarah broke the silence. "Richard, do you think James is happy in this relationship?"

Richard paused, considering her question carefully. "I'm not sure, Sarah," he admitted. "It's hard to say. But from what I've observed, there seems to be a genuine connection between them."

Sarah nodded thoughtfully. "It must be incredibly challenging for James to balance his feelings for David with his obligations to his family," she mused. Richard sighed, feeling a pang of empathy for his friend. "I can't even begin to imagine what he's going through," he confessed. "But I know he's struggling, and I want to do whatever I can to help."

Sarah squeezed Richard's hand reassuringly. "We'll be there for him, Richard," she said firmly. "Whatever he needs, we'll support him."

Richard offered her a grateful smile, feeling a sense of relief wash over him. With Sarah by his side, he felt more equipped to navigate the complexities of their friend's situation.

As they continued to discuss their approach to supporting James, Richard felt a renewed sense of determination. No matter the challenges, he knew that he and Sarah would face them together, united in their commitment to be there for their friend.

In the following days, Richard made a conscious effort to reach out to James, offering him a listening ear and a shoulder to lean on. He knew that James was navigating uncharted territory and wanted to be there for him every step of the way.

Their conversations were filled with moments of vulnerability and honesty as James shared the intricacies of his relationship with David and the challenges he faced in his personal life. Richard listened with empathy, offering words of encouragement and understanding.

Meanwhile, Sarah provided her support from afar, offering words of wisdom and encouragement over the phone. She reminded Richard to be patient and compassionate, urging him to give James the space and time he needed to work through his emotions.

As the weeks passed, Richard and Sarah's support proved invaluable to James, helping him navigate the complexities of his relationship with David and find solace amidst the turmoil of his personal life.

Through it all, Richard and Sarah remained steadfast in their commitment to their friend, offering unwavering support and understanding as he embarked on this journey of self-discovery and growth. In doing so, they strengthened their bond with James, forging a friendship that would endure time.

As the project of refurbishing the house in Notting Hill neared its completion, every detail seemed to take on a newfound significance. Richard, James, and David poured their hearts and souls into the final touches, ensuring that every aspect of the house was perfect down to the smallest detail.

The walls were painted in soft, neutral tones, creating a sense of warmth and tranquillity throughout the space. Light fixtures adorned the ceilings, casting a soft glow that illuminated every corner of the room. The floors, meticulously polished to a high shine, gleamed underfoot, reflecting the light and adding to the overall spaciousness.

In the kitchen, sleek, modern appliances starkly contrasted the classic, timeless design. Quartz countertops sparkled in the sunlight, while custom-built cabinets provided ample storage space for all the essentials. A large island served as the centrepiece of the room, offering a gathering place for family and friends to come together and share meals.

In the living room, plush sofas and armchairs beckoned invitingly, their soft cushions offering a cosy place to relax and unwind. A fireplace stood against one wall, its crackling flames adding warmth and ambience to the space. Bookshelves lined the walls, filled with an eclectic mix of novels, photographs, and decorative objects that spoke to the family's unique personality and interests.

Upstairs, the bedrooms were havens of comfort and serenity, each one carefully designed to reflect the individual tastes of its occupants. Soft, luxurious bedding adorned the beds, while large windows let in plenty of natural light. In the master bedroom, a king-sized bed took centre stage, its plush mattress promising a restful night's sleep.

Outside, the garden was a verdant oasis of greenery and tranquillity. Flower beds burst with colour, while a neatly trimmed lawn provided the perfect backdrop for outdoor gatherings and al fresco dining. A stone patio offered a place to relax and soak up the sun, while a bubbling fountain added a soothing soundtrack to the scene.

As the final touches were put in place and the last coat of paint applied, Richard, James, and David couldn't help but feel a sense of pride and accomplishment. The house had been transformed into a true masterpiece, reflecting their hard work, dedication, and unwavering commitment to excellence.

As the final weeks of the refurbishing project in Notting Hill unfolded, the Thornton family paid a visit to the house to inspect the progress. Richard, James and David stood nervously as Mr. and Mrs. Thornton entered, their eyes scanning the room with eager anticipation.

To their relief and delight, the Thorntons' faces broke into smiles as they took in the transformation that had taken place. Mrs.

Thornton clasped her hands together in joy while Mr. Thornton nodded approvingly, his eyes twinkling with satisfaction.

"It's even better than we imagined," Mrs. Thornton exclaimed, her voice filled with genuine excitement. "You've done an incredible job, Richard."

Mr. Thornton echoed her sentiments, adding, "The attention to detail is truly remarkable. You've captured exactly what we were hoping for."

Richard, James, and David breathed a collective sigh of relief, knowing that their hard work and dedication were finally paying off. They eagerly showed the Thorntons around the house, pointing out each carefully crafted detail and explaining the thought process behind their design choices.

As they moved from room to room, the Thorntons' smiles grew more expansive, their enthusiasm infectious. They marvelled at the kitchen, admired the cosy living room, and expressed their delight at the bedrooms upstairs. Outside, they wandered through the garden, admiring the lush greenery and vibrant blooms.

"It's perfect," Mrs. Thornton declared as they made their way back inside. "We couldn't be happier."

Mr Thornton nodded in agreement. "Indeed," he said. "You've exceeded our expectations in every way."

Richard, James, and David beamed with pride, their hearts swelling with satisfaction at the Thorntons' words of praise. It was a moment they would cherish forever—the culmination of months of hard work and dedication and the beginning of a new chapter for the house in Notting Hill.

With the refurbishing project in its final stages and the Thornton family delighted with the outcome, Richard began to contemplate his return to Bath. The prospect of being reunited with his family, particularly amidst the challenges they were facing with their teenagers, weighed heavily on his mind.

As the day drew to a close, the construction site buzzed with activity, the sounds of machinery and voices echoing through the air. It was in this bustling atmosphere that James's ex-wife unexpectedly made her appearance.

Her arrival sent a ripple of tension through the air, her presence casting a shadow over the otherwise busy scene. With furrowed brows and a determined expression, she approached the construction site foreman, her eyes scanning the area in search of James.

It didn't take long for her to realise that something was amiss. James was nowhere to be found, and the foreman's hesitant response only fuelled her growing unease.

Determined to get to the bottom of things, she pressed the foreman for answers; her voice tinged with urgency. "Where's James?" she demanded, her tone brooking no room for evasion.
The foreman hesitated, casting a wary glance around the site before reluctantly admitting the truth. "I'm not sure, ma'am," he replied, his voice tinged with apprehension. "He hasn't been here for the past few nights."

Her heart pounding in her chest, James's ex-wife felt a surge of panic wash over her. Where could he be? What could he be doing that would keep him away from his responsibilities at a time like this?

Determined to find answers, she searched for James, her footsteps quickening with each passing moment. Little did she know that her quest for the truth would lead her down a path she never imagined. She noticed that James was not there, and without answers, she went home but returned the next day.

The following afternoon, as the sun began its descent toward the horizon, Emily returned to the construction site, her resolve unwavering despite the tumultuous emotions swirling inside her.

James spotted her from across the site, his heart sinking as he braced for another confrontation. He exchanged a tense glance with David, who stood nearby, his expression a mixture of concern and apprehension.

As Emily approached, her footsteps echoing against the concrete floor, James swallowed hard, steeling himself for the conversation that was sure to follow.

"Emily," he greeted her cautiously, his voice tinged with uncertainty. "I wasn't expecting to see you again so soon."

Emily's expression softened slightly at the sound of his voice, though her eyes remained guarded. "I needed to talk to you," she replied, her tone more subdued than before.

James nodded, gesturing toward a nearby bench where they could speak privately. "Of course," he said, leading her away from the hustle and bustle of the construction site.

As they settled onto the bench, an uneasy silence descended between them, punctuated only by the distant sounds of machinery and the occasional shout of a construction worker.

Finally, Emily broke the silence, her voice hesitant yet determined. "James, I... I need to know what's going on," she began, her words tumbling out in a rush. "I need to understand why you've been avoiding me, why you've been spending so much time away from home."

James shifted uncomfortably under her gaze, struggling to find the right words to explain his actions. "Emily, I... I didn't mean to shut you out," he began, his voice tinged with regret. "It's just... things have been difficult lately, and I needed some space to figure things out."

Emily's brow furrowed in confusion, her eyes searching his face for answers. "Difficult, how?" she pressed, her tone softening slightly. "Is it because of us? Because of our marriage?"

James hesitated, grappling with how much to reveal. "It's complicated," he admitted, his voice barely above a whisper. "There are things I need to sort out, things I need to figure out on my own."

Emily's expression softened at his words, her heart aching at the pain she saw in his eyes. "James, you don't have to do this alone," she said gently, reaching out to take his hand in hers. "We're in this together, remember? For better or for worse."

James squeezed her hand tightly, gratitude flooding through him at her words. "I know," he said quietly, a sense of relief washing over him. "And I'm sorry for shutting you out. I promise we'll figure this out together."

With that, they sat in silence, the weight of their shared struggles hanging heavy in the air between them. But despite the challenges ahead, James felt a glimmer of hope, knowing that Emily was by his side, ready to face whatever the future held together.

As they started arguing and Emily lost her temper, screaming her frustrations, David appeared at the scene, drawn by the commotion. His eyes widened in surprise as he took in the tense atmosphere, sensing the underlying tension between James and his ex-wife.

"Is everything okay here?" David interjected, his voice calm but concerned.

James glanced at David, grateful for his presence but also wary of the situation unfolding before them. "It's fine, David," he replied, attempting to diffuse the tension. "Just a misunderstanding."

But Emily's anger had reached its boiling point, and she turned her fury on David. "Who are you, anyway?" she demanded, her voice dripping with disdain. "And why are you interfering in our conversation?"

David held up his hands in a placating gesture, his expression remaining neutral despite Emily's hostility. "I'm David," he reiterated, his tone steady. "I work with James on the construction project. We're just trying to resolve this peacefully."

Emily scoffed, her frustration bubbling over. "Peacefully?" she echoed, her voice tinged with sarcasm. "There's nothing peaceful about this situation, David. My ex-husband is lying to me, and you're covering for him."

James stepped forward, attempting to defuse the situation before it escalated further. "Emily, please," he pleaded, his tone tinged with regret. "Let's talk about this calmly."

But Emily was beyond reason, her anger consuming her rationality. "I don't want to talk to you, James," she spat, her voice trembling with emotion. "And I certainly don't want to talk to your little friend here."

With that, she stormed away, leaving James and David standing in her wake, the weight of her words lingering in the air like a bitter echo. As they watched her retreat, a sense of unease settled over them, knowing that the confrontation was far from over.

James sighed heavily, running a hand through his hair in frustration as he watched Emily disappear into the distance. He felt a mixture of anger, guilt, and helplessness swirling inside him, knowing that he had hurt her deeply but unsure of how to mend the rift between them.

David placed a reassuring hand on James's shoulder, offering silent support in the face of the turmoil. "I'm sorry, James,"he said softly, his voice tinged with sympathy. "I didn't mean to make things worse."

James shook his head, the weight of the situation bearing down on him. "It's not your fault, David," he replied, his tone heavy with resignation. "This was bound to happen sooner or later."

As they stood there in the fading light of the evening, the construction site suddenly felt eerily quiet, the bustling activity of earlier now replaced by a palpable tension. James couldn't shake the feeling of unease that lingered in the air, knowing that his personal life had spilt over into his professional world in a way he hadn't anticipated.

With a heavy heart, James turned to David, his expression filled with resignation. "I think it's time we called it a day," he said wearily. There's nothing more we can do here tonight."

David nodded in agreement, understanding the need to retreat and regroup after the confrontation with Emily. Together, they gathered their tools and equipment, the weight of the evening's events hanging heavy in the air as they prepared to leave the construction site behind for the night.

Richard watched from a distance, his heart heavy with empathy for James but unsure how to offer support without overstepping boundaries. As James and David dealt with the aftermath of Emily's outburst, Richard chose to remain quiet, recognising that this was a situation that he couldn't fix with words alone.

Instead, he focused on his tasks, keeping himself busy with the remaining work on the construction site. With each hammer blow and nail driven, he tried to push aside the nagging thoughts and worries that threatened to consume him.

But despite his efforts to distract himself, Richard couldn't shake the feeling of unease that settled over him like a dark cloud. He knew that James was hurting, and part of him longed to reach out and offer comfort. Yet, he also understood the delicate nature of the situation and the need to respect James's privacy.

And so, Richard continued to work in silence, his mind filled with thoughts of what could have been and the uncertainty of what lay ahead. He knew the road ahead would be difficult for James, but he also believed that his friend had the strength to weather the storm, even if he couldn't see it himself.

Richard felt a sense of resignation wash over him as the sun dipped below the horizon, casting long shadows across the construction site. For now, all he could do was stand by and offer silent support, trusting that James would find his way through the darkness in his own time.

In the days that followed Emily's unexpected appearance, tensions on the construction site remained palpable. James seemed more withdrawn than usual, his usual easygoing demeanour overshadowed by the weight of his personal struggles. David, too, appeared preoccupied, his ordinarily jovial nature muted as he grappled with the fallout from Emily's confrontation.

Richard observed their interactions with a heavy heart, wishing there was something more he could do to ease their burdens. Yet, he knew that this was a battle they would have to fight on their terms. Still, he couldn't shake the feeling of helplessness that gnawed at him, a silent witness to the turmoil around him.

As the project neared completion, Richard found himself between a desire to finish the job and a growing sense of unease about the unresolved

tensions simmering beneath the surface. He longed for the day when the
construction site would be a place of joy and accomplishment rather than a battleground for his friends' emotional turmoil.

But despite their challenges, Richard remained steadfast in his commitment to see the project through to the end. He poured his energy into his work each day, channelling his frustrations and fears into the task. Richard felt pride in what they had accomplished together as the final touches were put in place and the last coat of paint applied.

As the construction site transformed into a beautiful home, Richard couldn't help but feel hope for the future. Though the road ahead would undoubtedly be fraught with challenges, he knew that with the support of friends like James and David, they could weather any storm that came their way.

As they stood together in the newly renovated house, Richard felt a renewed sense of optimism wash over him. Though the scars of the past would always remain, he knew they had emerged more robust and resilient than ever before. As they looked ahead to the future, Richard couldn't help but believe that brighter days were on the horizon.

CHAPTER 7

FINAL PROJECT AND HOUSE CONCLUSION

❖

As the days passed, the final touches were added to the refurbished house in Notting Hill. Richard and James worked tirelessly alongside their team, and their dedication and expertise were evident in every detail. Finally, after months of hard work and commitment, the project was complete.

The house owners arrived for the final inspection, their eyes lighting up with delight as they stepped through the door. They marvelled at the transformation, from the sleek modern design to the meticulous attention to detail.

"We couldn't be happier," Mr. Thornton exclaimed, his voice filled with genuine appreciation. "You've truly outdone yourselves."

Richard and James exchanged proud smiles, their hard work finally paying off to the client's satisfaction. It was a moment of triumph, a validation of their talent and dedication to their craft.

As Mr. and Mrs. Thornton explored each room, their excitement palpable, Richard and James stood back, watching with pride as their vision came to life before their eyes. The gleaming hardwood floors, the freshly painted walls, and the carefully curated furnishings all spoke to the care and expertise that had gone into the renovation.

"It's like a whole new house," Mrs. Thornton exclaimed, her eyes sparkling with delight.

Richard nodded, a sense of satisfaction washing over him. "We wanted to create a space that felt both modern and inviting," he explained. "Somewhere you could truly feel at home."

Mrs. Thornton beamed, her appreciation evident. "You've more than succeeded," she said warmly. "This is beyond anything we could have imagined."

As they made their way through the house, Richard and James pointed out various features and design elements, eager to share their passion for the project. The Thorntons listened intently, their enthusiasm growing with each new detail.

When they reached the small room on the ground floor, the mood shifted to solemn reflection. This room, transformed into a mini-museum, honoured Elizabeth Hawkins. Featuring her restored paintings, copies of Reed's diary entries, and historical artefacts from the period, the space also included a plaque telling Elizabeth's story and the circumstances of her untimely death.

Mr Thornton spoke softly, "This was one of the biggest challenges we faced. Discovering the mystery bones and uncovering Elizabeth's story added a profound layer to this house. We felt a responsibility to her memory."

Mrs. Thornton nodded, her eyes misting slightly. "Transforming this room into a memorial space was about preserving history and giving Elizabeth a voice and a place in our home. It's deeply moving to see it all come together."

Richard and James exchanged a glance of shared pride and respect, understanding the significance of their work beyond mere renovation.

The sun began to set when they reached the garden, casting a warm golden glow over the lush greenery. The Thorntons stood in awe, taking in the serene beauty of the outdoor space.

"It's like a little oasis in the heart of the city," Mr. Thornton remarked, his voice filled with wonder.

Richard and James exchanged a satisfied glance, knowing they had achieved their goal of creating a sanctuary where the Thorntons could escape the hustle and bustle of London life.

Richard and James felt a sense of accomplishment wash over them as they bid farewell to the happy homeowners. The months of hard work and dedication had paid off, culminating in a project that had not only met but exceeded their client's expectations.

As they watched the Thorntons drive away, Richard and James couldn't help but feel a swell of pride in what they had achieved. It was a moment they would carry with them for years, a reminder of the transformative power of passion, dedication, and a shared vision.

Just as they began to gather their tools and prepare to leave, Mr. Thornton's voice called out from the driveway. "Richard, James, wait just a moment!"

Curious, the two men approached, their brows furrowed in confusion. Mr. Thornton leaned out of the car window, a mischievous twinkle in his eye.

"We've decided to give you both a little gift," he announced, a grin spreading across his face.

"We're giving you ten extra days to enjoy the house before we move in!"

Richard and James exchanged astonished glances, their surprise quickly turning to delight. The Thorntons had made an unexpected gesture of gratitude, one that they were only too happy to accept.

"Thank you," Richard exclaimed, his voice filled with genuine appreciation. "That's incredibly generous of you."

Mr. Thornton waved off their thanks with a chuckle. "Consider it a small token of our appreciation for all your hard work," he said warmly. "You've earned it."

With that, the Thorntons drove off once more, leaving Richard and James standing in the driveway, their hearts full of gratitude.

As they watched the car disappear around the corner, Richard and James couldn't help but feel a surge of excitement at the prospect of spending a few more days in the beautiful house they had worked so hard to create.

With renewed energy and enthusiasm, they gathered their belongings and made plans for the days ahead. It was a rare opportunity to enjoy the fruits of their labour, and they intended to make the most of every moment.

As the sun dipped below the horizon, casting a warm golden glow over the streets of Notting Hill, Emily's unexpected arrival sent a ripple of tension through the tranquil evening. James tensed as he saw her approaching, her expression wrought with anger and frustration.
"James!" she called out, her voice cutting through the quiet of the evening. "We need to talk."

James exchanged a wary glance with Richard, a knot of apprehension forming in his stomach. With a resigned sigh, he stepped forward to meet Emily, bracing himself for the inevitable confrontation.

"What do you want, Emily?" he asked, his tone guarded.

Emily's eyes flashed with fury as she stopped in front of him, her hands clenched into fists at her sides. "I want the truth, James," she demanded, her voice trembling with emotion. "I want to know what's going on."

James hesitated, his gaze flicking nervously towards Richard before returning to Emily. He knew that he couldn't keep lying to her, that she deserved to know the truth, no matter how painful it might be.

Taking a deep breath, he summoned the courage to speak, his voice barely above a whisper. "I... I've been keeping something from you, Emily," he admitted, his words heavy with regret.
Emily's eyes widened in surprise, her anger momentarily forgotten as she waited for him to continue.

"It's about David," James continued, his voice faltering slightly. "And me."

Emily's brow furrowed in confusion, her mind racing as she tried to make sense of his words. "What do you mean?" she asked, her voice barely a whisper.

James took a shaky breath, steeling himself for her reaction. "I... I'm in love with him, Emily," he confessed, the words tumbling out in a rush.

"David and I... we're together."

Emily's breath caught in her throat as his words sank in. Her heart shattered into a million pieces as the truth washed over her; she felt as if the ground had been ripped out from beneath her, leaving her suspended in a void of disbelief and despair.

Tears welled up in her eyes as she struggled to find the words to respond, her emotions swirling in a turbulent storm of hurt and betrayal.

James watched her reaction with a heavy heart, his own eyes brimming with tears as he realised the pain he had caused her.

"I'm so sorry, Emily," he whispered, reaching out to touch her arm. "I never wanted to hurt you."

But Emily recoiled from his touch, her heartache too raw to bear. With a choked sob, she turned on her heel and fled into the gathering darkness, leaving James standing alone on the empty street, his world shattered by the weight of his confession.

As Emily's words pierced the air like a dagger, James felt a wave of despair wash over him, his heart breaking at the pain he had caused her. He watched helplessly as she unleashed her fury, her voice echoing through the quiet streets of Notting Hill.

"You're a disgrace, James!" she spat, her words laced with venom. "A shame to our family! Everyone will know what you've done, and you'll never see your daughter again!"

James felt as if the ground had been torn out from beneath him, his world crumbling around him as he faced the devastating consequences of his actions. The weight of Emily's words pressed down on him like a heavy burden, suffocating him with guilt and remorse.

He wanted to reach out to her and plead for forgiveness, but he knew it was too late. He had crossed a line that could never be undone, and now he would have to live with the consequences for the rest of his life.

As Emily stormed away into the night, her words echoing in his ears, James felt a sense of emptiness wash over him, a hollow ache that seemed to consume him from the inside out. He had lost everything – his marriage, his family, and perhaps worst of all, himself.

With a heavy heart, James turned and walked away, the weight of his mistakes weighing heavily on his shoulders. He knew he could never undo the pain he had caused, but perhaps, in time, he could find a way to make amends and rebuild what he had lost.

But for now, all he could do was face the consequences of his actions and try to find a way to live with the shattered remnants of his life.

James's mind was a whirlwind of emotions as he walked away from the scene. Guilt, regret, and sorrow consumed him, each step heavier than the last as he grappled with the magnitude of his actions.

He found himself wandering the familiar streets of Notting Hill, the vibrant neighbourhood now shrouded in darkness and shadow. Everywhere he looked, he was reminded of the life he had built here – the memories, the moments of joy and laughter, now tainted by the betrayal he had wrought.

Lost in his thoughts, James wandered until he found himself standing before the refurbished house, bathed in the soft glow of streetlights. It stood as a testament to his talent and dedication, symbolising everything he had worked hard to achieve.

But now, as he gazed up at the familiar facade, he couldn't help but feel a sense of emptiness. The house, once a source of pride and accomplishment, now served as a painful reminder of everything he had lost.

With a heavy heart, James turned away from the house and continued down the quiet streets, his footsteps echoing in the silence of the night. He didn't know where he was going or what the future held, but one thing was sure – his life would never be the same again.

As dawn broke on the horizon, James found himself at a crossroads, faced with the daunting task of rebuilding his shattered life. It would be a long and arduous journey, filled with challenges and obstacles, but he was determined to face it head-on.

With a newfound sense of resolve, James took a deep breath and began to walk forward, one step at a time, into the unknown. And as he disappeared into the morning light, he knew that no matter what lay ahead, he would face it with courage and determination, ready to embrace whatever the future held.

Having witnessed the turmoil and distress plaguing James, David resolved to offer his unwavering support during this challenging time. As the sun rose on a new day, David sought out James, determined to provide a comforting presence amidst the chaos.

With a gentle hand on James' shoulder, David offered a reassuring smile, silently conveying his solidarity and steadfast support. "I'm here for you, James," he said softly, his voice laced with empathy. "Whatever you need, whatever you're going through, I'll be by your side."

James met David's gaze, gratitude and relief flooding his weary heart. In David's presence, he found solace and strength, a reminder that he wasn't alone in his struggles.
Together, they walked side by side, navigating the uncertain path ahead with courage and resilience. With David's unwavering support guiding him, James felt a flicker of hope ignite, a glimmer of light in the darkness of his despair.

In the days that followed, David remained a steadfast presence in James' life, offering a listening ear, a shoulder to lean on, and unwavering support through every twist and turn of their journey. And as they faced the challenges ahead together, James knew that with David by his side, he could overcome anything.

As James grappled with the aftermath of his confrontation with Emily, David stood by his side, offering a comforting presence and a sympathetic ear. They retreated to the quiet solitude of David's home, seeking refuge from the storm of emotions that raged within them.

In the safety of David's embrace, James found the courage to confront his fears and doubts. He shared the depths of his anguish, the weight of his guilt, and the uncertainty that gnawed at his soul. And with each word he spoke, David listened with unwavering compassion, offering encouragement and understanding.

Together, they navigated the tumultuous waters of James' emotions, finding solace in each other's company. David's steadfast support became a beacon of light in the darkness, guiding James through the darkest nights and offering hope for a brighter tomorrow.

As the days passed, James found strength in David's presence, his resolve bolstered by the unwavering support of his friend. And though the road ahead remained uncertain, James knew that with David by his side, he could face whatever challenges.

Their bond deepened with each passing day, forged in the crucible of adversity and tempered by the fires of shared experience. And as they stood together, facing the trials of life with courage and resilience, James knew that their friendship was a gift to be cherished forevermore.

As Richard contemplated his next steps, he found solace in his friends' familiar embrace. They gathered at a local pub, the warmth of camaraderie washing over them like a comforting blanket.

Amidst the laughter and chatter, Richard shared his decision to leave the house behind and return to his life in Bath. His friends listened attentively, offering encouragement and support as he grappled with the weight of his choices.

With each sip of his drink, Richard found clarity amid uncertainty. He imparted sage advice to his friends, drawing from his experiences and insights gleaned from a lifetime of trials and triumphs.

As the evening wore on, Richard's spirits lifted, buoyed by his friends' unwavering support. He knew that whatever challenges lay ahead, he would face them with courage and resilience, fortified by the bonds of friendship that bound them together.

And as they raised their glasses in a toast to new beginnings, Richard felt a sense of peace wash over him. Though the road ahead was uncertain, he knew that with his friends by his side, he could weather any storm that came his way.

As they walked away from the house, their heads held high and their hearts full, Richard and James knew they had left their mark on Notting Hill and each other. The echoes of their laughter and the memories of their shared triumphs lingered in the air, a testament to the bond they had forged amidst the construction chaos.

Though their journey together may have ended, the lessons they had learned and the experiences they had shared would stay with them forever. They had faced challenges and obstacles with unwavering determination, emerging stronger and more resilient each day.

As they turned the corner and disappeared into the bustling streets of London, Richard and James knew that their paths would diverge, leading them in different directions. But the memories they had created and the bonds they had forged would endure, a testament to the power of friendship and the strength of the human spirit.

Their footsteps echoed softly against the pavement; a rhythmic cadence mirrored their hearts' beat. They walked in silence, each lost in their thoughts, yet bound together by the shared journey they had embarked upon.

Richard glanced over at James, his gaze filled with gratitude and fondness. In James, he had found not just a colleague but a friend, a confidant who had stood by his side through the trials and triumphs of the past months.

James returned the look with a smile, his eyes reflecting the warmth of their shared memories. In Richard, he had found not just a mentor but a kindred spirit—a companion who had shared his joys and sorrows and helped him find his way when he had lost his path.

As they reached the end of the street, they paused, their eyes lingering on the familiar sight of the bustling cityscape. At that moment, they knew that their journey together had come to an end. But as they parted ways, they carried the indelible mark of their shared experience, a bond that would endure long after they said their goodbyes.

With a final nod of acknowledgement, Richard and James went their separate ways, their hearts filled with gratitude for their shared journey and hope for the adventures ahead. And as they disappeared into the city's embrace, they knew they would always carry a piece of Notting Hill with them wherever they went.

Richard returned to the familiar streets of Bath, his heart heavy with the weight of the memories he had made in Notting Hill. As he settled back into his routine, he found solace in the familiar rhythms of daily life, the comforting embrace of his family, the gentle laughter of his children, and the quiet beauty of the countryside that surrounded them.

Meanwhile, James and David returned to their home in London, their hearts still echoing with the bittersweet melody of their shared experience. As they stepped through the door of their cosy apartment, the warmth of familiarity greeted them, the soft purring of Lissa, the cat, the delicate scent of orchids that filled the air, and the reassuring presence of each other.

Though they had left Notting Hill behind, the memories of their time there lingered as a constant reminder of the bonds they had formed and the lessons they had learned. As they embarked on the next chapter of their lives, they carried with them the knowledge that no matter where their paths may lead, they would always be connected by the shared journey they had undertaken together.

ABOUT THE AUTHOR

The author, Edi Gonzalo, assumes full responsibility for the content of this work, which was published by Vividart Studios in partnership with Amazon.

Edi Gonzalo photography

Edi Gonzalo is a Luso-Brazilian writer, blending the rich cultural heritage of both Portugal and Brazil in his storytelling. Having moved to London, the author portrays the reality of the city based on spring experiences and encounters with Londoners and world citizens who, for various reasons, crossed his path and shared their stories. The named individuals have some relation to the author. He currently lives in London, enjoying a lifelong affair with books.

Instagram: @edi.sampa
Facebook: @Edigonzalo

At Vividart Studios, we bring your ideas to life with our insightful touch. Our journey is filled with stories, inspiration, and creativity, all designed to spark your imagination. Whether

VividArt Studios

YOUR IDEAS, OUR INSIGHTFUL TOUCH

you're looking to unwind, explore your artistic side, or find a unique gift, our books and colouring books are perfect for all ages and interests. Dive into a world of intricate designs and let your creativity flow. Join us and discover the joy of colouring with Vividart Studios.

We invite you to continue your literary journey by exploring our collection of books. Discover new perspectives, unlock fresh stories, and add more hues to your imagination.

Printed in Great Britain
by Amazon